Lyra's journey north will continue in

THE GOLDEN COMPASS
THE GRAPHIC NOVEL

VOLUME 2 coming in September 2016 and

VOLUME 3 coming in September 2017

HIS DARK MATERIALS

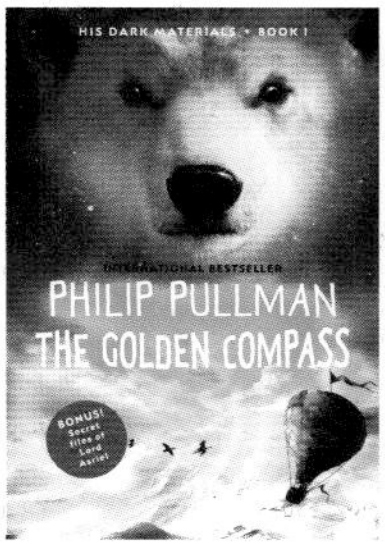
PHILIP PULLMAN
THE GOLDEN COMPASS

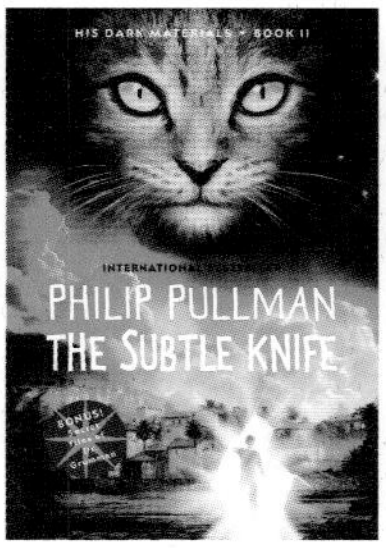
PHILIP PULLMAN
THE SUBTLE KNIFE

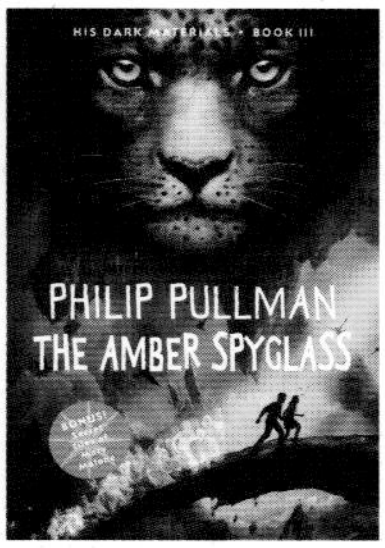
PHILIP PULLMAN
THE AMBER SPYGLASS

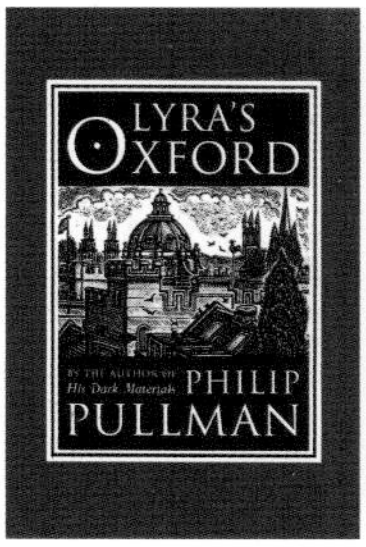
LYRA'S OXFORD
PHILIP PULLMAN

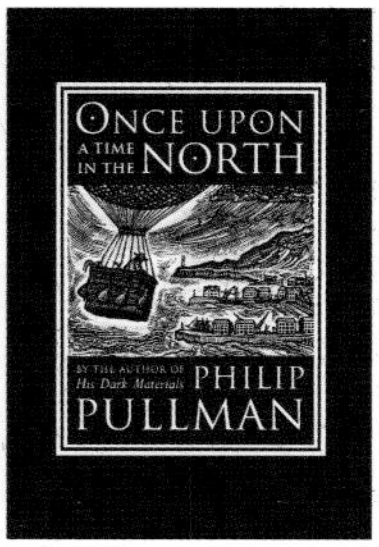
ONCE UPON A TIME IN THE NORTH
PHILIP PULLMAN

"Pullman's imagination soars. . . . A literary rollercoaster ride you won't want to miss." —*The Boston Globe*

"A literary masterpiece. . . . The most magnificent fantasy series since The Lord of the Rings." —*The Oregonian*

"Pullman is quite possibly a genius . . . using the lineaments of fantasy to tell the truth about the universal experience of growing up." —*Newsweek*

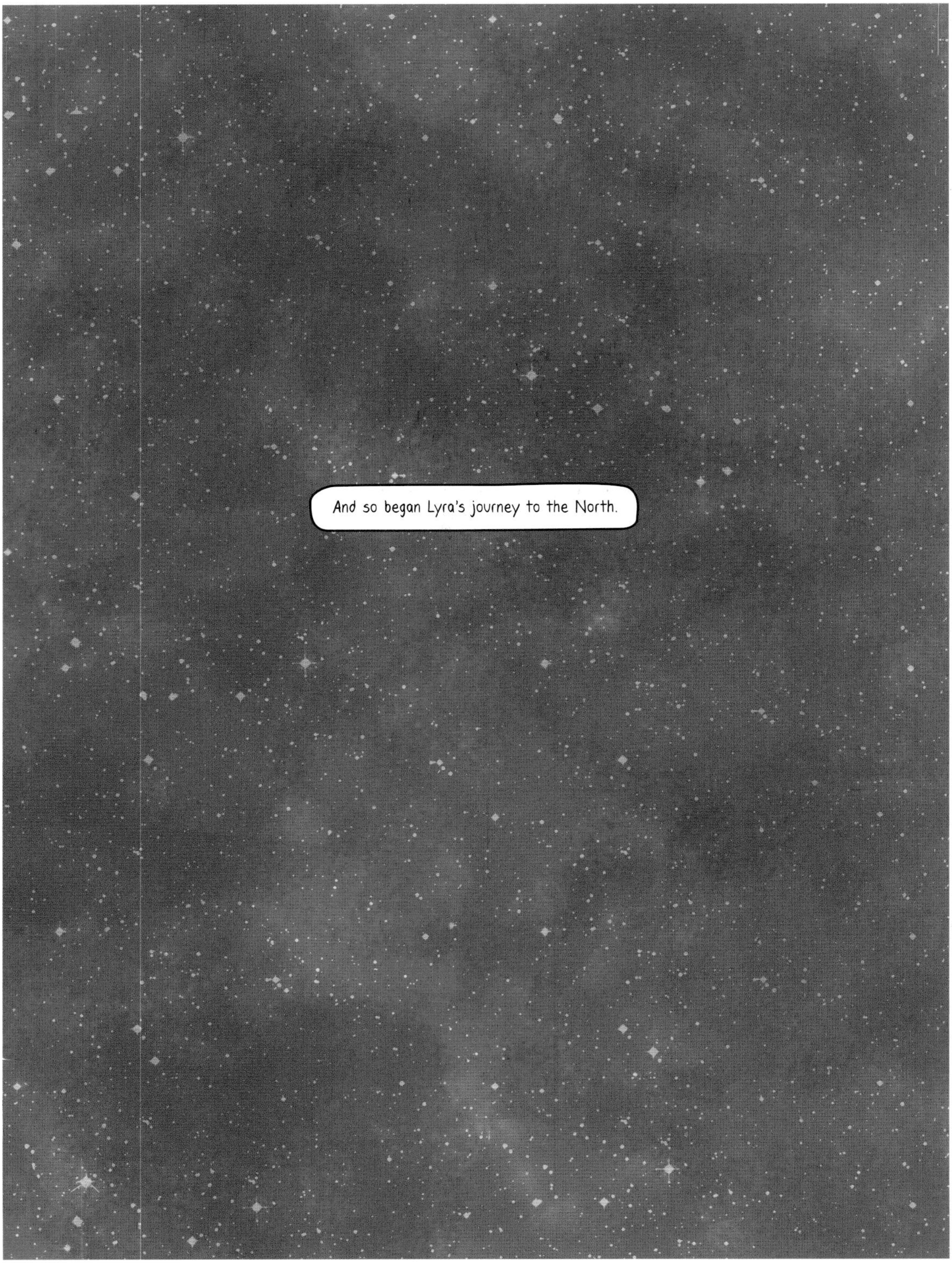
And so began Lyra's journey to the North.

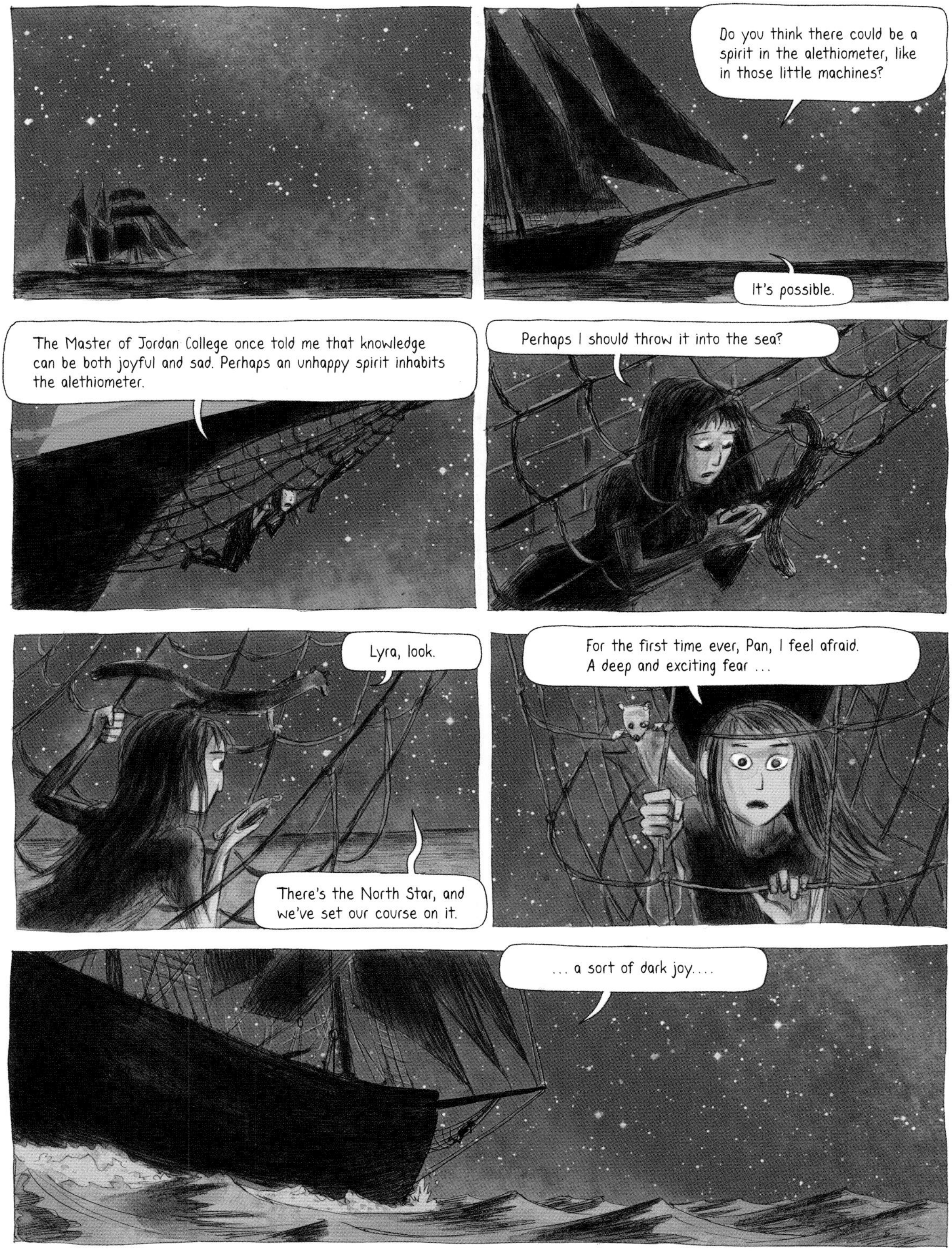
Do you think there could be a spirit in the alethiometer, like in those little machines?
It's possible.
The Master of Jordan College once told me that knowledge can be both joyful and sad. Perhaps an unhappy spirit inhabits the alethiometer.
Perhaps I should throw it into the sea?
Lyra, look.
There's the North Star, and we've set our course on it.
For the first time ever, Pan, I feel afraid. A deep and exciting fear ...
... a sort of dark joy....

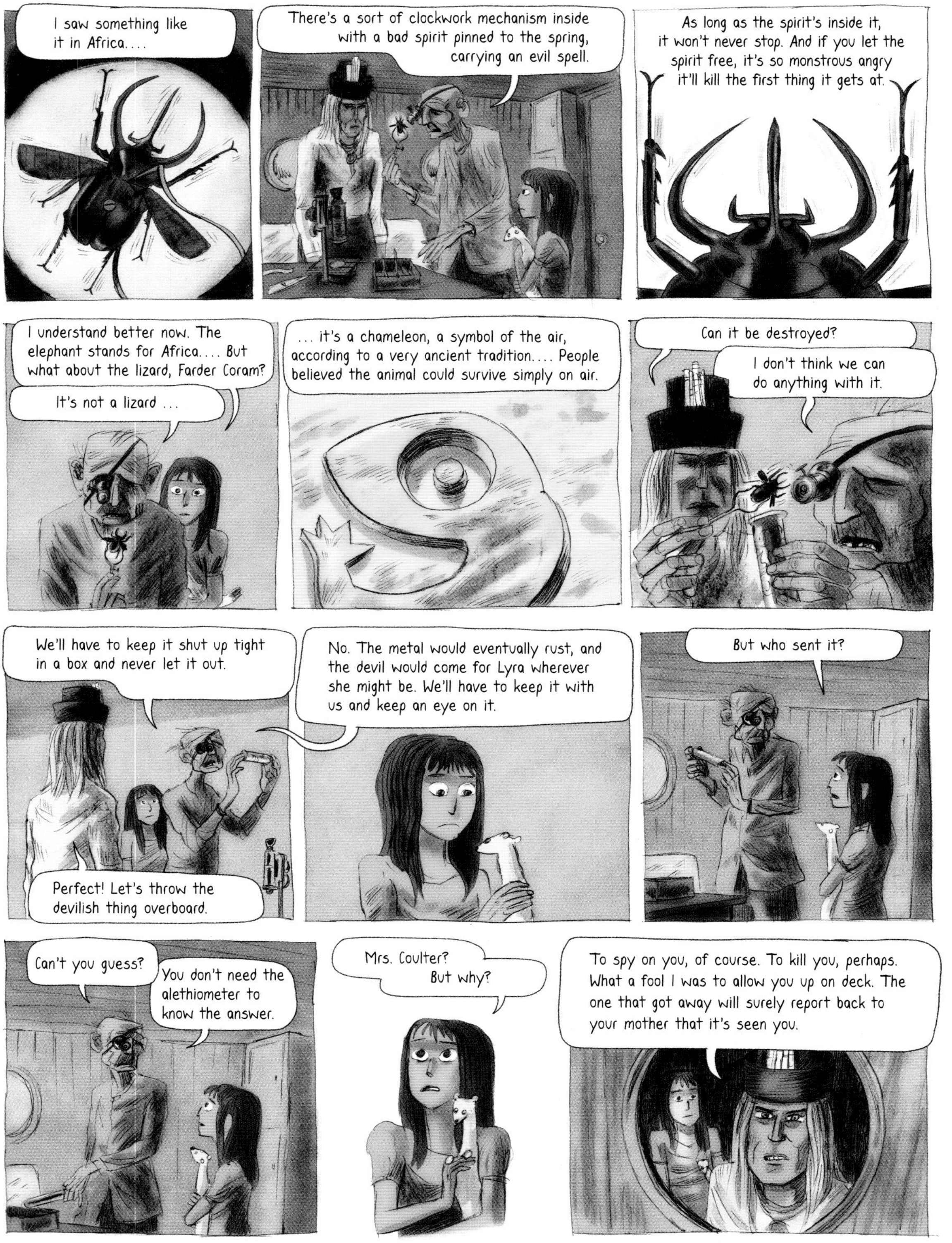
I saw something like it in Africa....
There's a sort of clockwork mechanism inside with a bad spirit pinned to the spring, carrying an evil spell.
As long as the spirit's inside it, it won't never stop. And if you let the spirit free, it's so monstrous angry it'll kill the first thing it gets at.
I understand better now. The elephant stands for Africa.... But what about the lizard, Farder Coram?
It's not a lizard ...
... it's a chameleon, a symbol of the air, according to a very ancient tradition.... People believed the animal could survive simply on air.
Can it be destroyed?
I don't think we can do anything with it.
We'll have to keep it shut up tight in a box and never let it out.
Perfect! Let's throw the devilish thing overboard.
No. The metal would eventually rust, and the devil would come for Lyra wherever she might be. We'll have to keep it with us and keep an eye on it.
But who sent it?
Can't you guess?
You don't need the alethiometer to know the answer.
Mrs. Coulter? But why?
To spy on you, of course. To kill you, perhaps. What a fool I was to allow you up on deck. The one that got away will surely report back to your mother that it's seen you.

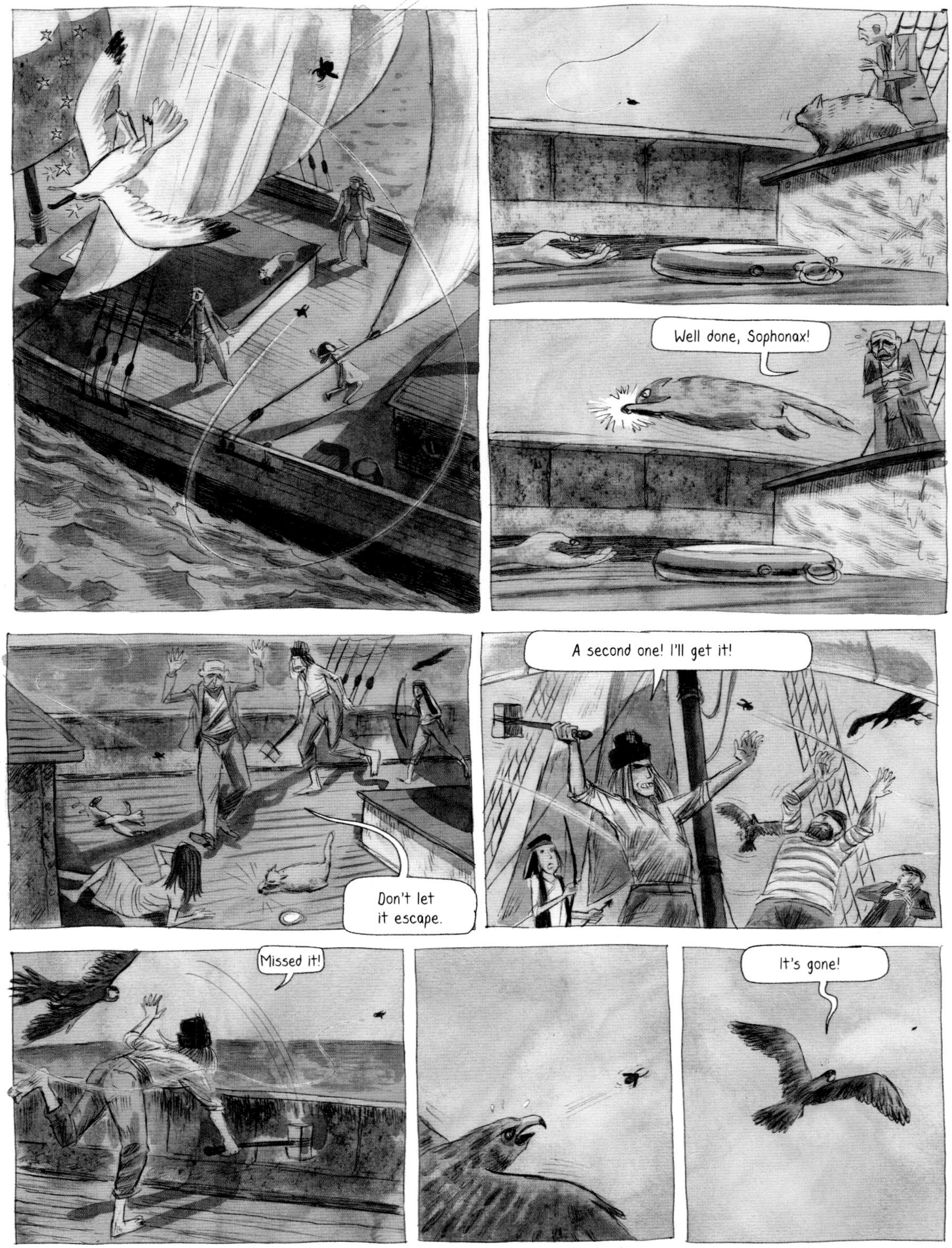
Well done, Sophonax!
Don't let it escape.
A second one! I'll get it!
Missed it!
It's gone!

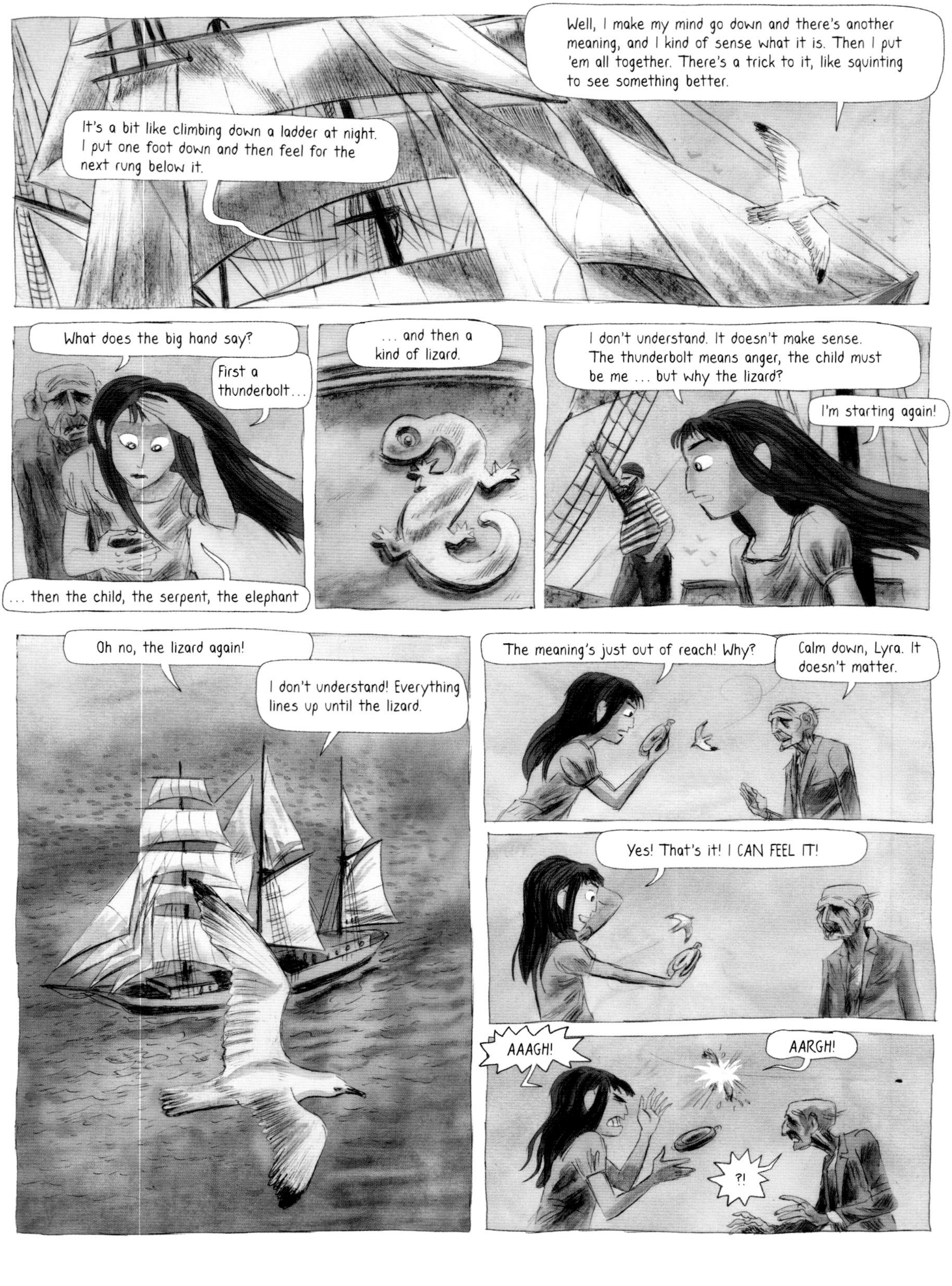
Well, I make my mind go down and there's another meaning, and I kind of sense what it is. Then I put 'em all together. There's a trick to it, like squinting to see something better.
It's a bit like climbing down a ladder at night. I put one foot down and then feel for the next rung below it.
What does the big hand say?
First a thunderbolt . . .
. . . then the child, the serpent, the elephant
. . . and then a kind of lizard.
I don't understand. It doesn't make sense. The thunderbolt means anger, the child must be me . . . but why the lizard?
I'm starting again!
Oh no, the lizard again!
I don't understand! Everything lines up until the lizard.
The meaning's just out of reach! Why?
Calm down, Lyra. It doesn't matter.
Yes! That's it! I CAN FEEL IT!
AAAGH!
AARGH!
?!

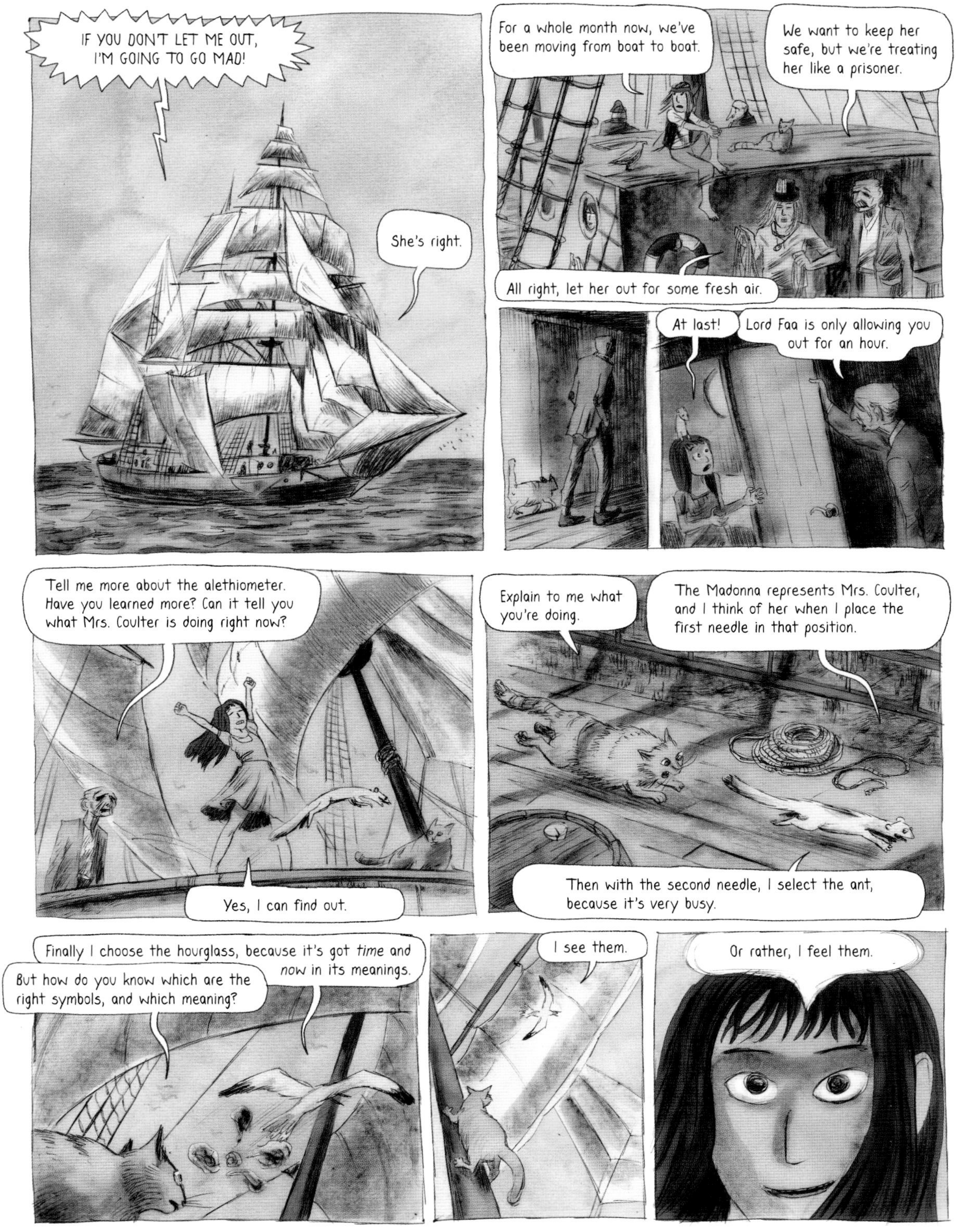
IF YOU DON'T LET ME OUT, I'M GOING TO GO MAD!
She's right.
For a whole month now, we've been moving from boat to boat.
We want to keep her safe, but we're treating her like a prisoner.
All right, let her out for some fresh air.
At last!
Lord Faa is only allowing you out for an hour.
Tell me more about the alethiometer. Have you learned more? Can it tell you what Mrs. Coulter is doing right now?
Yes, I can find out.
Explain to me what you're doing.
The Madonna represents Mrs. Coulter, and I think of her when I place the first needle in that position.
Then with the second needle, I select the ant, because it's very busy.
Finally I choose the hourglass, because it's got *time* and *now* in its meanings.
But how do you know which are the right symbols, and which meaning?
I see them.
Or rather, I feel them.

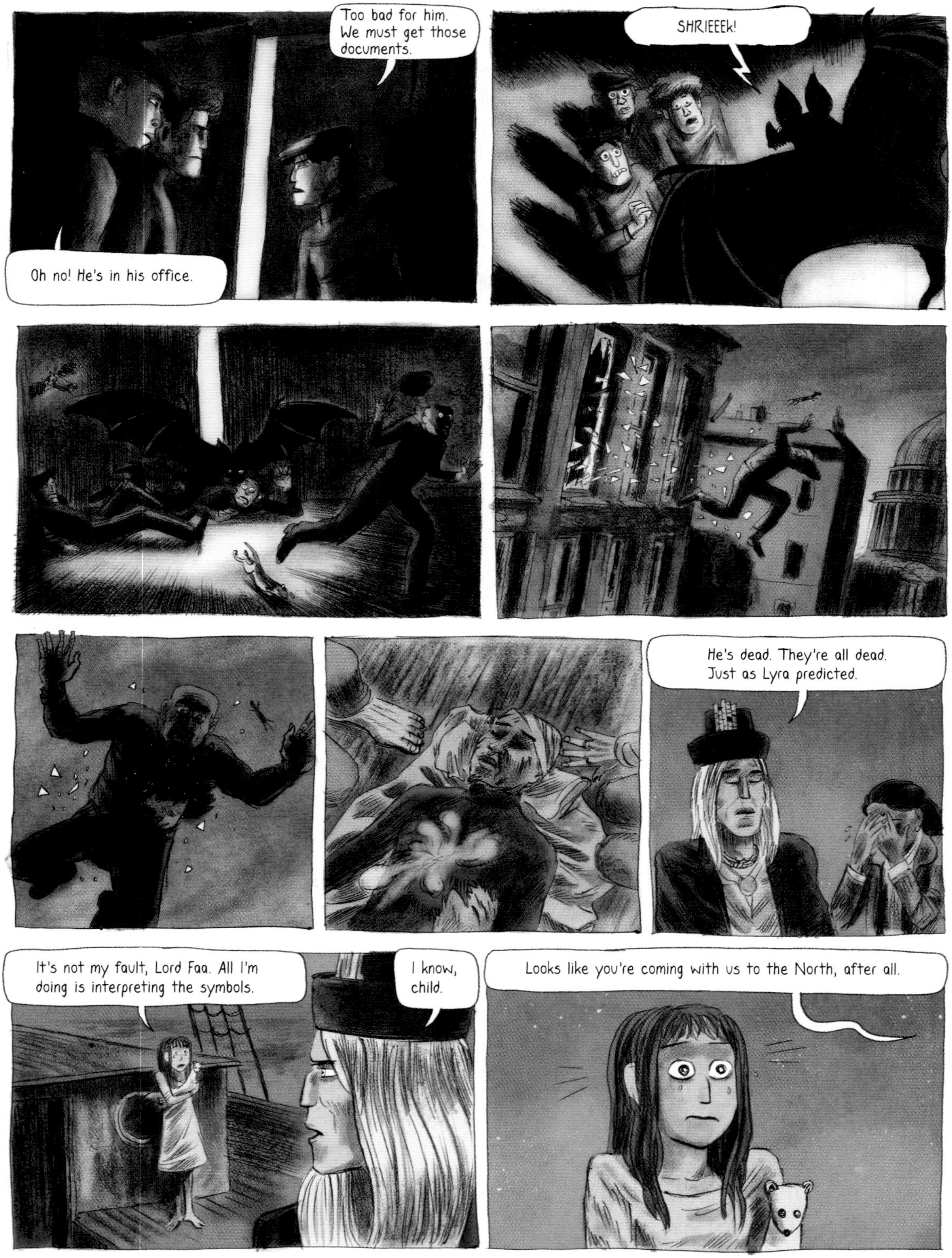
Too bad for him. We must get those documents.
Oh no! He's in his office.
SHRIEEEk!
He's dead. They're all dead. Just as Lyra predicted.
It's not my fault, Lord Faa. All I'm doing is interpreting the symbols.
I know, child.
Looks like you're coming with us to the North, after all.

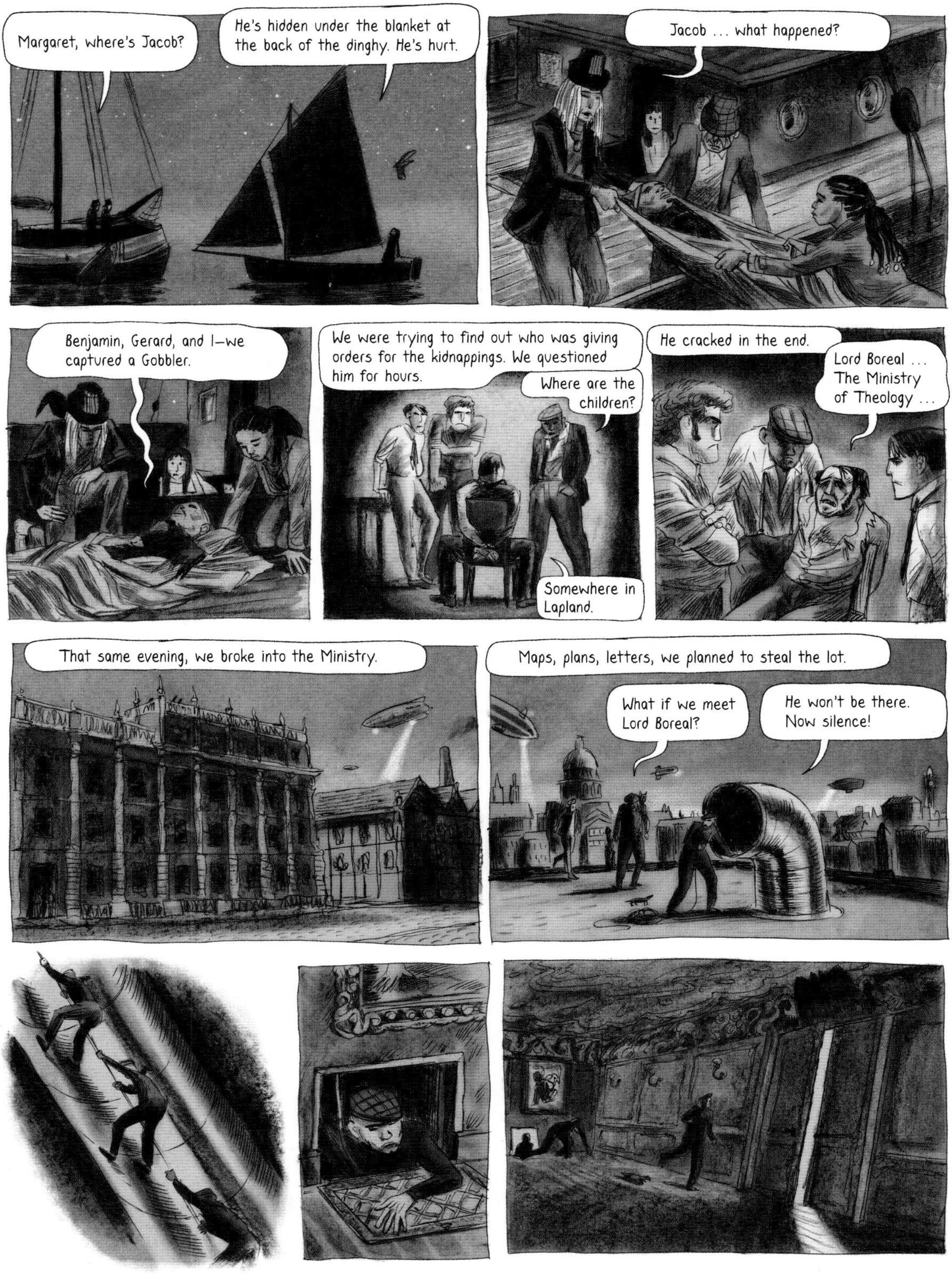
Margaret, where's Jacob?
He's hidden under the blanket at the back of the dinghy. He's hurt.
Jacob ... what happened?
Benjamin, Gerard, and I—we captured a Gobbler.
We were trying to find out who was giving orders for the kidnappings. We questioned him for hours.
Where are the children?
Somewhere in Lapland.
He cracked in the end.
Lord Boreal ... The Ministry of Theology ...
That same evening, we broke into the Ministry.
Maps, plans, letters, we planned to steal the lot.
What if we meet Lord Boreal?
He won't be there. Now silence!

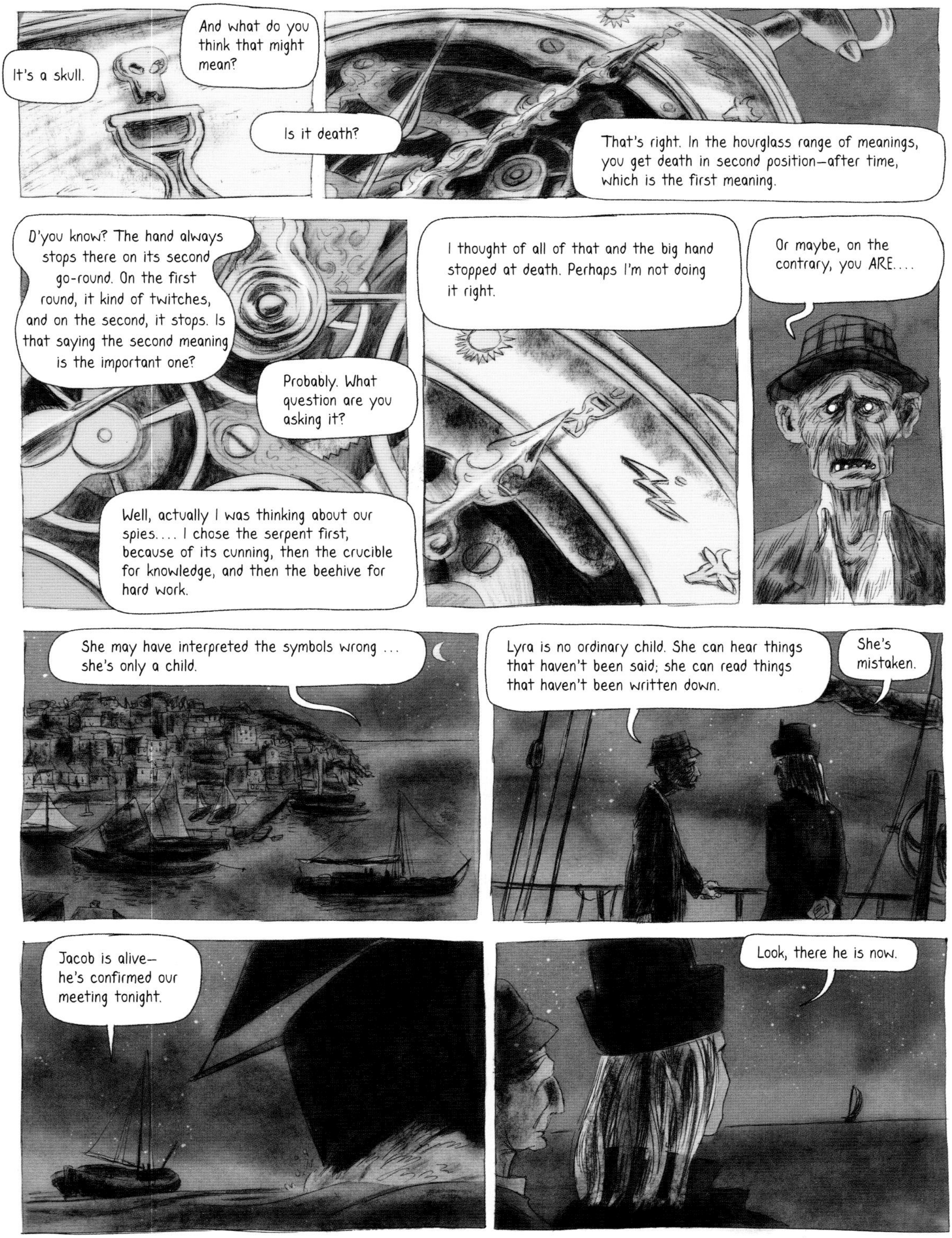
It's a skull.
And what do you think that might mean?
Is it death?
That's right. In the hourglass range of meanings, you get death in second position—after time, which is the first meaning.
D'you know? The hand always stops there on its second go-round. On the first round, it kind of twitches, and on the second, it stops. Is that saying the second meaning is the important one?
Probably. What question are you asking it?
Well, actually I was thinking about our spies.... I chose the serpent first, because of its cunning, then the crucible for knowledge, and then the beehive for hard work.
I thought of all of that and the big hand stopped at death. Perhaps I'm not doing it right.
Or maybe, on the contrary, you ARE....
She may have interpreted the symbols wrong ... she's only a child.
Lyra is no ordinary child. She can hear things that haven't been said; she can read things that haven't been written down.
She's mistaken.
Jacob is alive—he's confirmed our meeting tonight.
Look, there he is now.

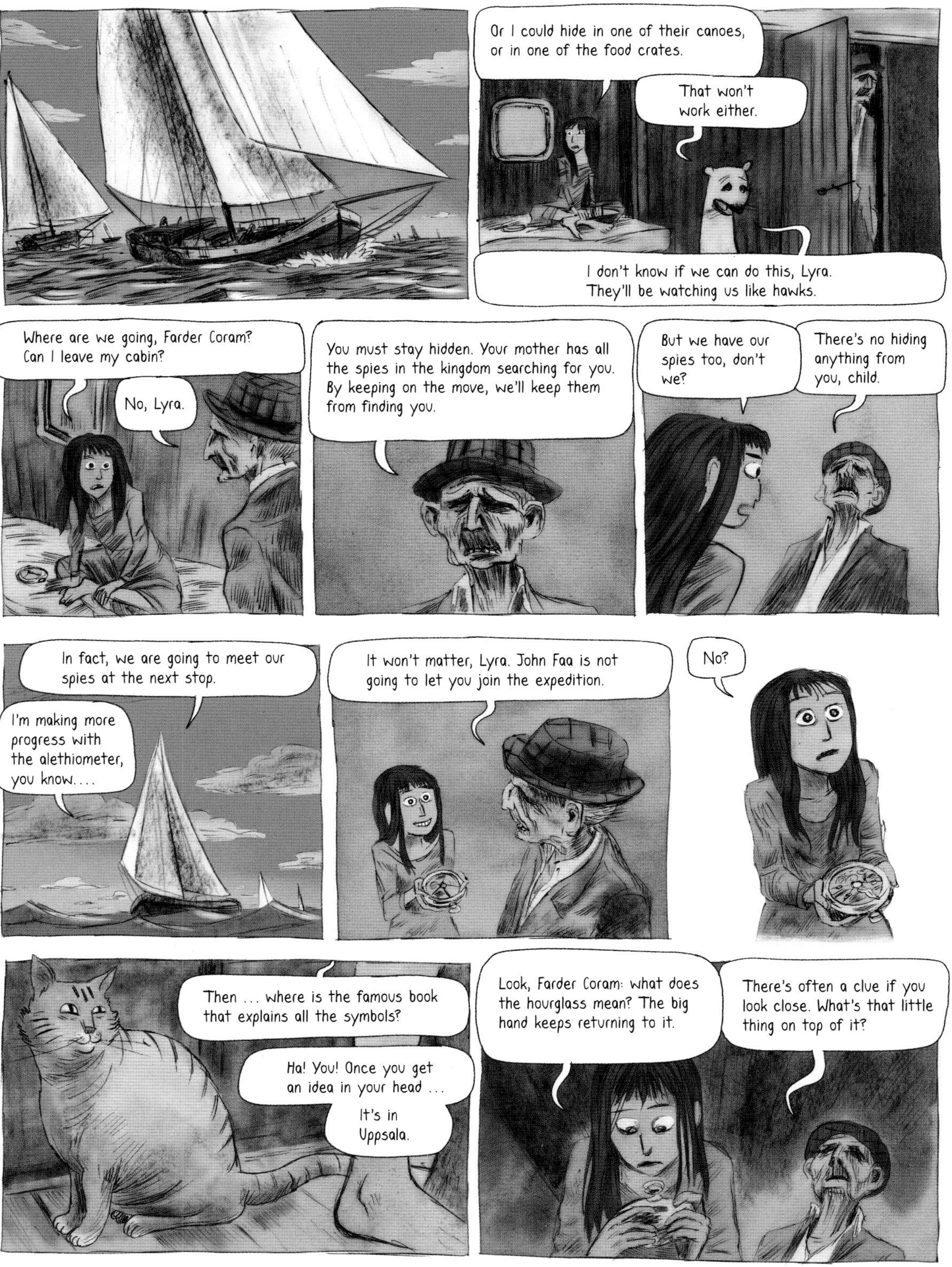
Or I could hide in one of their canoes, or in one of the food crates.
That won't work either.
I don't know if we can do this, Lyra. They'll be watching us like hawks.
Where are we going, Farder Coram? Can I leave my cabin?
No, Lyra.
You must stay hidden. Your mother has all the spies in the kingdom searching for you. By keeping on the move, we'll keep them from finding you.
But we have our spies too, don't we?
There's no hiding anything from you, child.
In fact, we are going to meet our spies at the next stop.
I'm making more progress with the alethiometer, you know. . . .
It won't matter, Lyra. John Faa is not going to let you join the expedition.
No?
Then . . . where is the famous book that explains all the symbols?
Ha! You! Once you get an idea in your head . . .
It's in Uppsala.
Look, Farder Coram: what does the hourglass mean? The big hand keeps returning to it.
There's often a clue if you look close. What's that little thing on top of it?

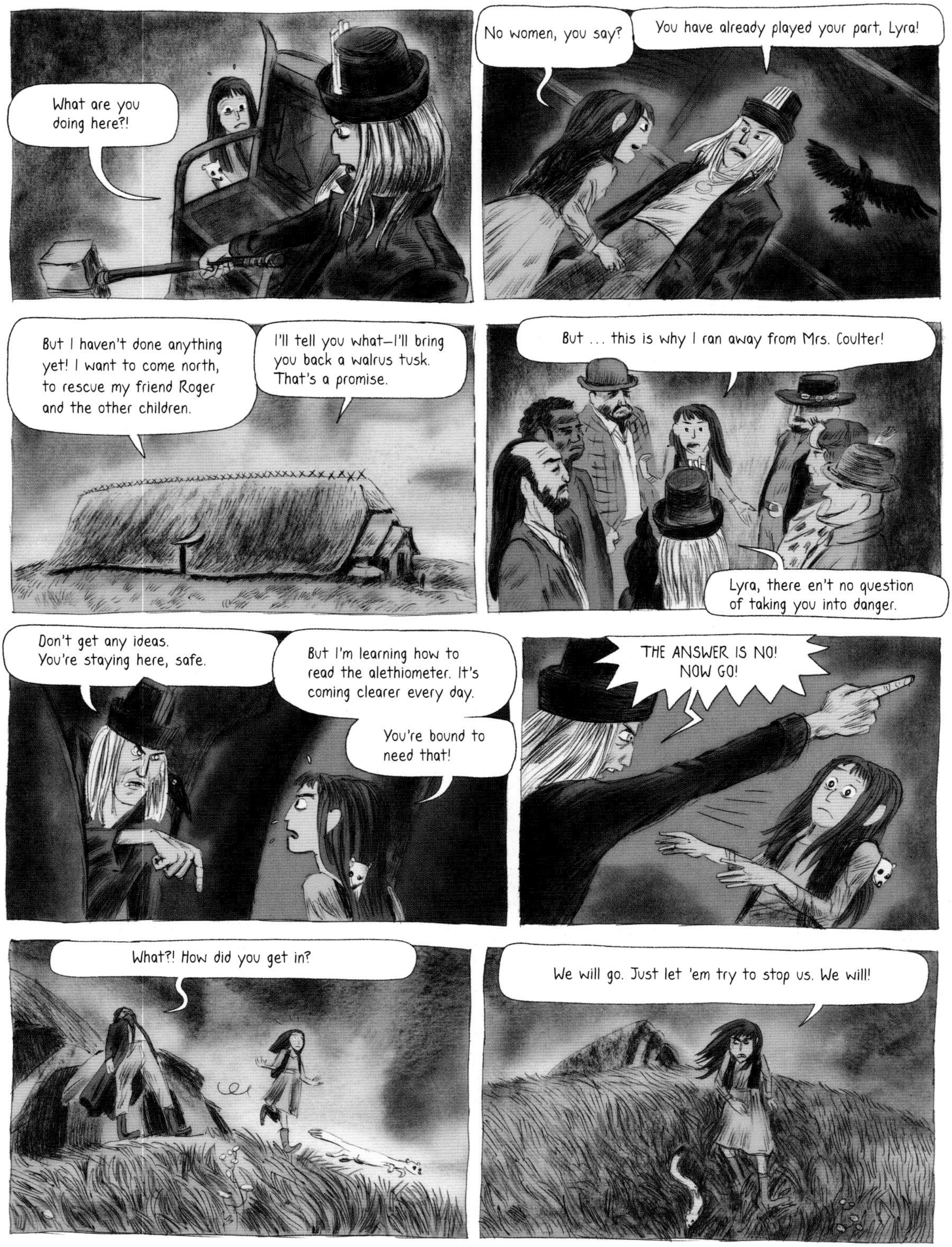
What are you doing here?!
No women, you say?
You have already played your part, Lyra!
But I haven't done anything yet! I want to come north, to rescue my friend Roger and the other children.
I'll tell you what—I'll bring you back a walrus tusk. That's a promise.
But ... this is why I ran away from Mrs. Coulter!
Lyra, there en't no question of taking you into danger.
Don't get any ideas. You're staying here, safe.
But I'm learning how to read the alethiometer. It's coming clearer every day.
You're bound to need that!
THE ANSWER IS NO! NOW GO!
What?! How did you get in?
We will go. Just let 'em try to stop us. We will!

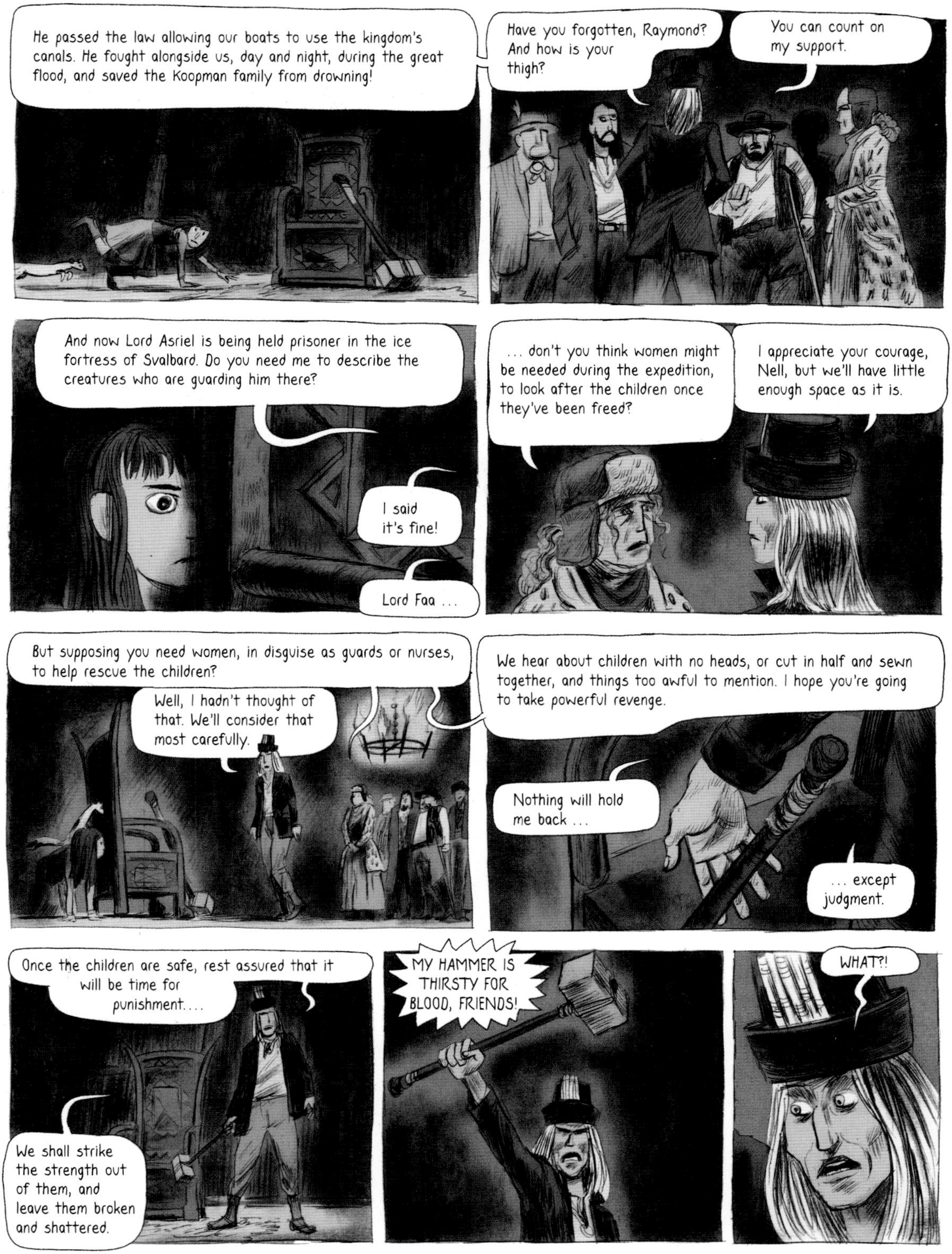
He passed the law allowing our boats to use the kingdom's canals. He fought alongside us, day and night, during the great flood, and saved the Koopman family from drowning!
Have you forgotten, Raymond? And how is your thigh?
You can count on my support.
And now Lord Asriel is being held prisoner in the ice fortress of Svalbard. Do you need me to describe the creatures who are guarding him there?
I said it's fine!
Lord Faa . . .
. . . don't you think women might be needed during the expedition, to look after the children once they've been freed?
I appreciate your courage, Nell, but we'll have little enough space as it is.
But supposing you need women, in disguise as guards or nurses, to help rescue the children?
Well, I hadn't thought of that. We'll consider that most carefully.
We hear about children with no heads, or cut in half and sewn together, and things too awful to mention. I hope you're going to take powerful revenge.
Nothing will hold me back . . .
. . . except judgment.
Once the children are safe, rest assured that it will be time for punishment. . . .
We shall strike the strength out of them, and leave them broken and shattered.
MY HAMMER IS THIRSTY FOR BLOOD, FRIENDS!
WHAT?!

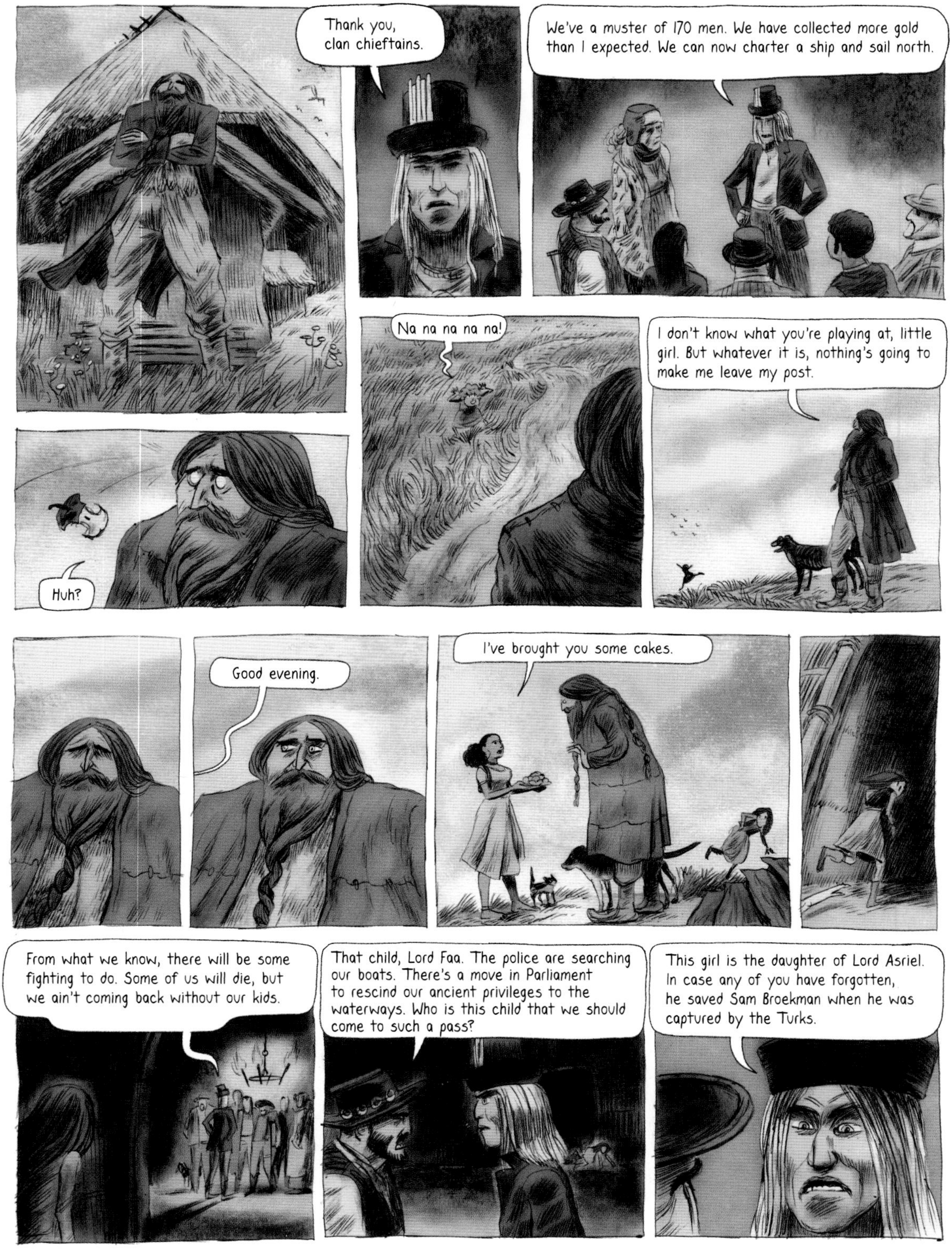
Thank you, clan chieftains.
We've a muster of 170 men. We have collected more gold than I expected. We can now charter a ship and sail north.
Huh?
Na na na na na!
I don't know what you're playing at, little girl. But whatever it is, nothing's going to make me leave my post.
Good evening.
I've brought you some cakes.
From what we know, there will be some fighting to do. Some of us will die, but we ain't coming back without our kids.
That child, Lord Faa. The police are searching our boats. There's a move in Parliament to rescind our ancient privileges to the waterways. Who is this child that we should come to such a pass?
This girl is the daughter of Lord Asriel. In case any of you have forgotten, he saved Sam Broekman when he was captured by the Turks.

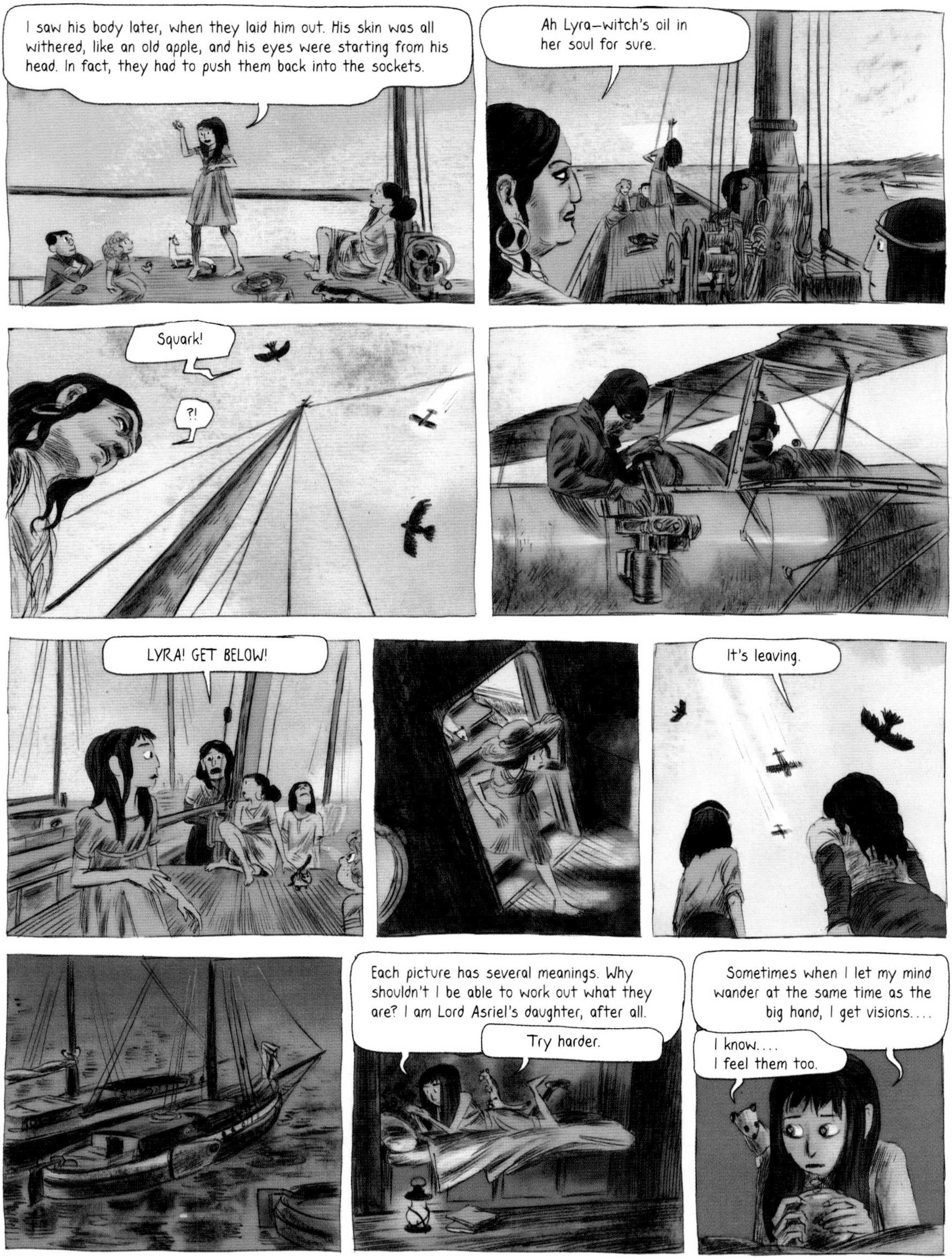
I saw his body later, when they laid him out. His skin was all withered, like an old apple, and his eyes were starting from his head. In fact, they had to push them back into the sockets.
Ah Lyra—witch's oil in her soul for sure.
Squark!
?!
LYRA! GET BELOW!
It's leaving.
Each picture has several meanings. Why shouldn't I be able to work out what they are? I am Lord Asriel's daughter, after all.
Try harder.
Sometimes when I let my mind wander at the same time as the big hand, I get visions....
I know....
I feel them too.

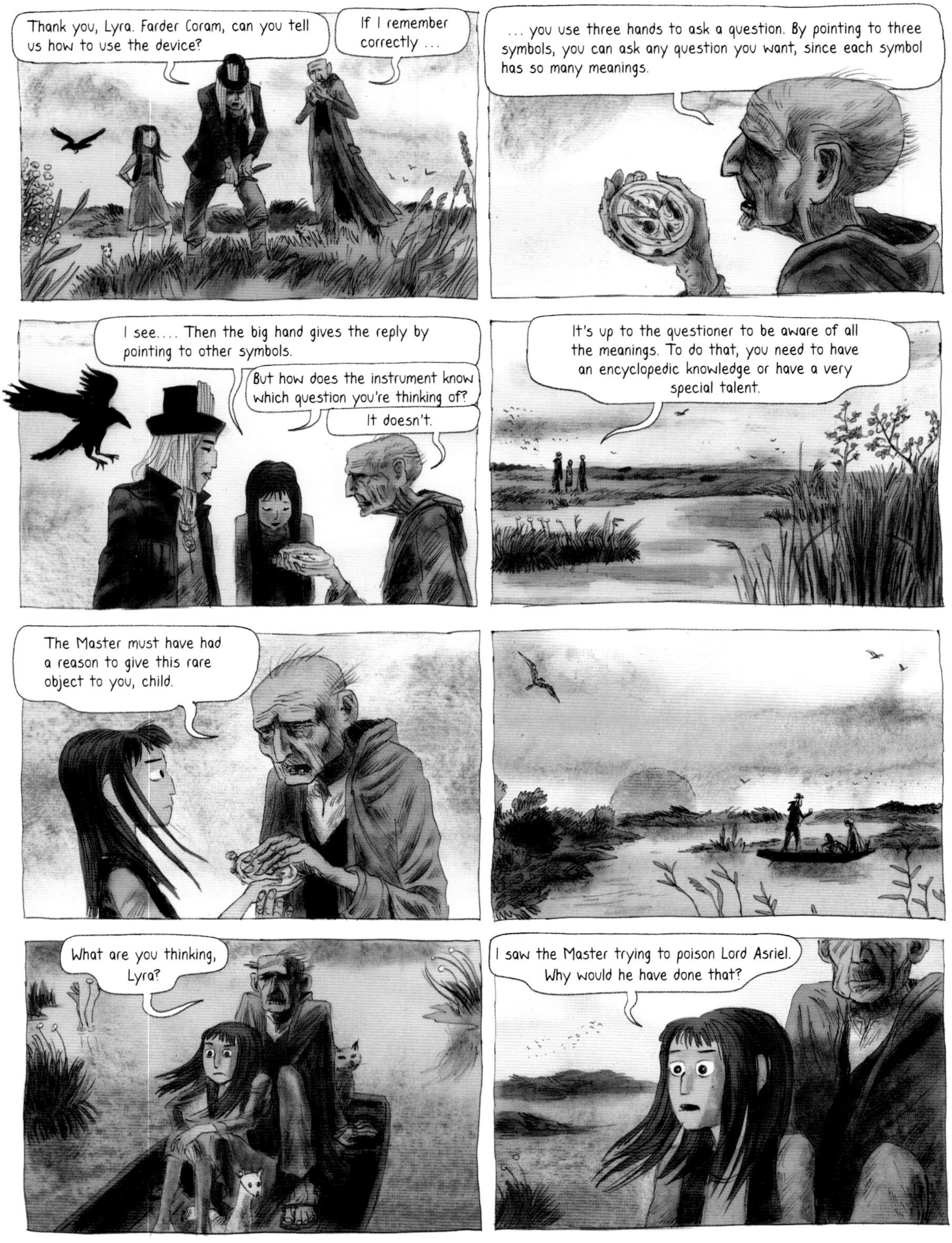
Thank you, Lyra. Farder Coram, can you tell us how to use the device?
If I remember correctly . . .
. . . you use three hands to ask a question. By pointing to three symbols, you can ask any question you want, since each symbol has so many meanings.
I see. . . . Then the big hand gives the reply by pointing to other symbols.
But how does the instrument know which question you're thinking of?
It doesn't.
It's up to the questioner to be aware of all the meanings. To do that, you need to have an encyclopedic knowledge or have a very special talent.
The Master must have had a reason to give this rare object to you, child.
What are you thinking, Lyra?
I saw the Master trying to poison Lord Asriel. Why would he have done that?

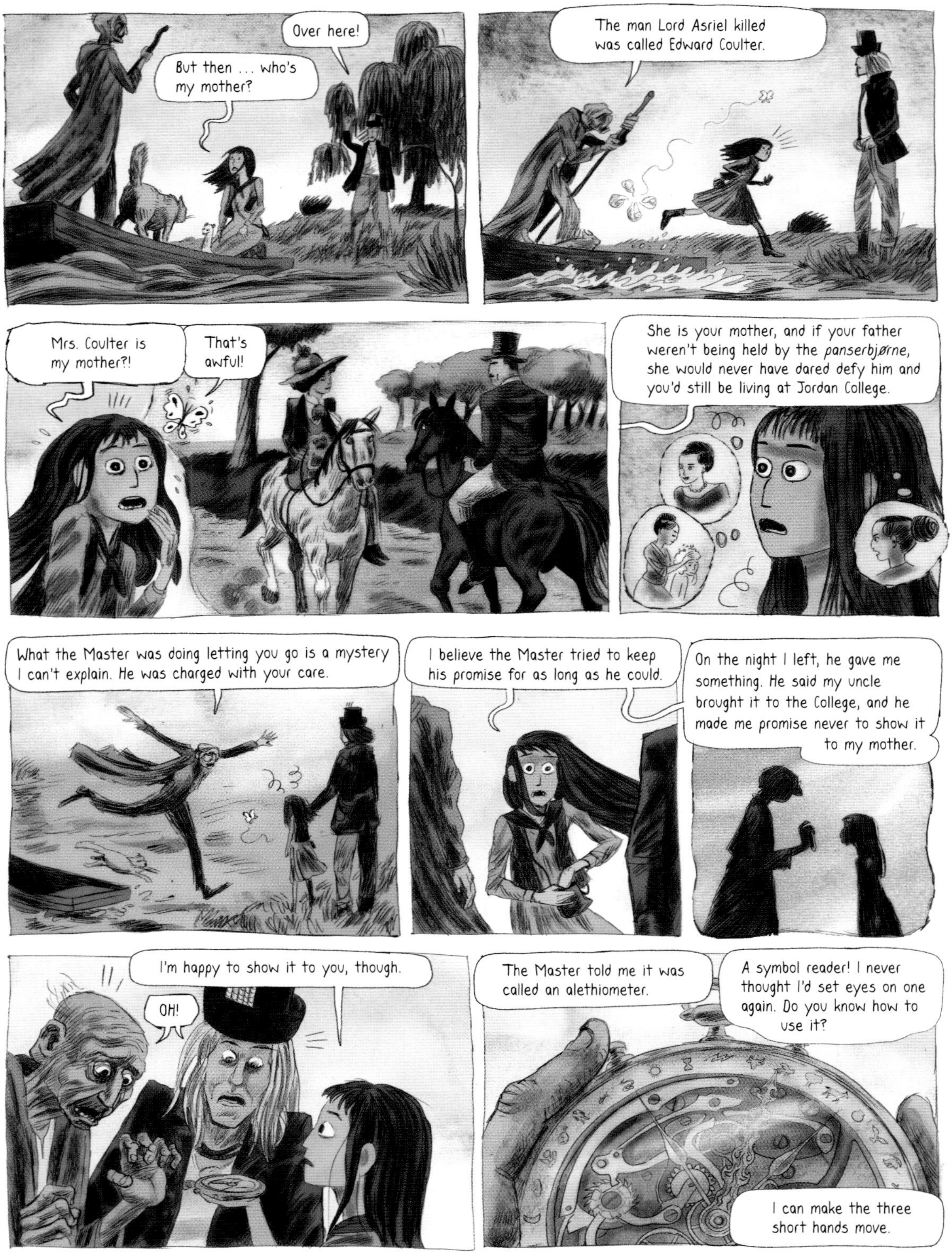
But then ... who's my mother?
Over here!
The man Lord Asriel killed was called Edward Coulter.
Mrs. Coulter is my mother?!
That's awful!
She is your mother, and if your father weren't being held by the *panserbjørne*, she would never have dared defy him and you'd still be living at Jordan College.
What the Master was doing letting you go is a mystery I can't explain. He was charged with your care.
I believe the Master tried to keep his promise for as long as he could.
On the night I left, he gave me something. He said my uncle brought it to the College, and he made me promise never to show it to my mother.
I'm happy to show it to you, though.
OH!
The Master told me it was called an alethiometer.
A symbol reader! I never thought I'd set eyes on one again. Do you know how to use it?
I can make the three short hands move.

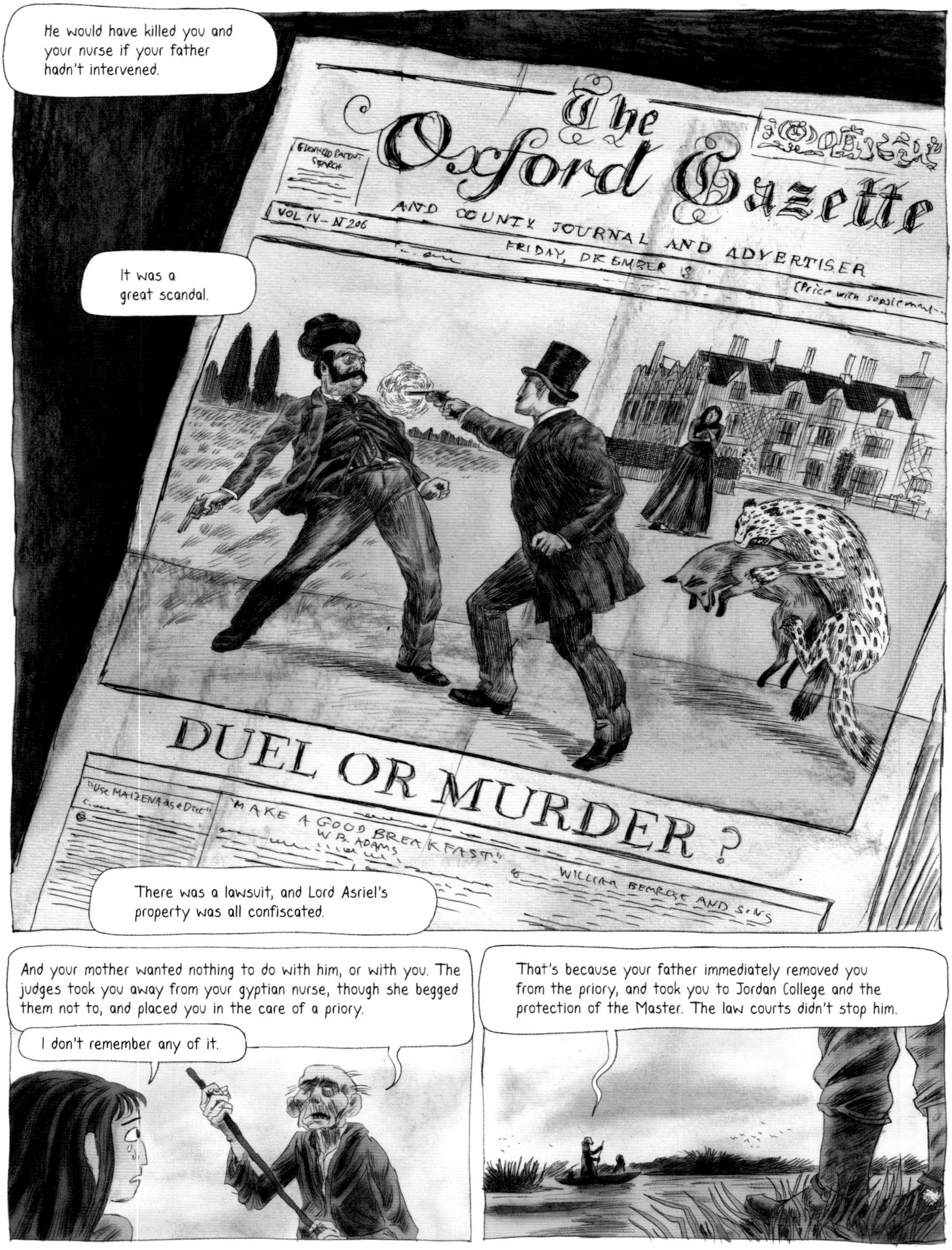
He would have killed you and your nurse if your father hadn't intervened.
The Oxford Gazette
AND COUNTY JOURNAL AND ADVERTISER
It was a great scandal.
DUEL OR MURDER?
"MAKE A GOOD BREAKFAST"
W.B. ADAMS
WILLIAM BEMROSE AND SONS
There was a lawsuit, and Lord Asriel's property was all confiscated.
And your mother wanted nothing to do with him, or with you. The judges took you away from your gyptian nurse, though she begged them not to, and placed you in the care of a priory.
I don't remember any of it.
That's because your father immediately removed you from the priory, and took you to Jordan College and the protection of the Master. The law courts didn't stop him.

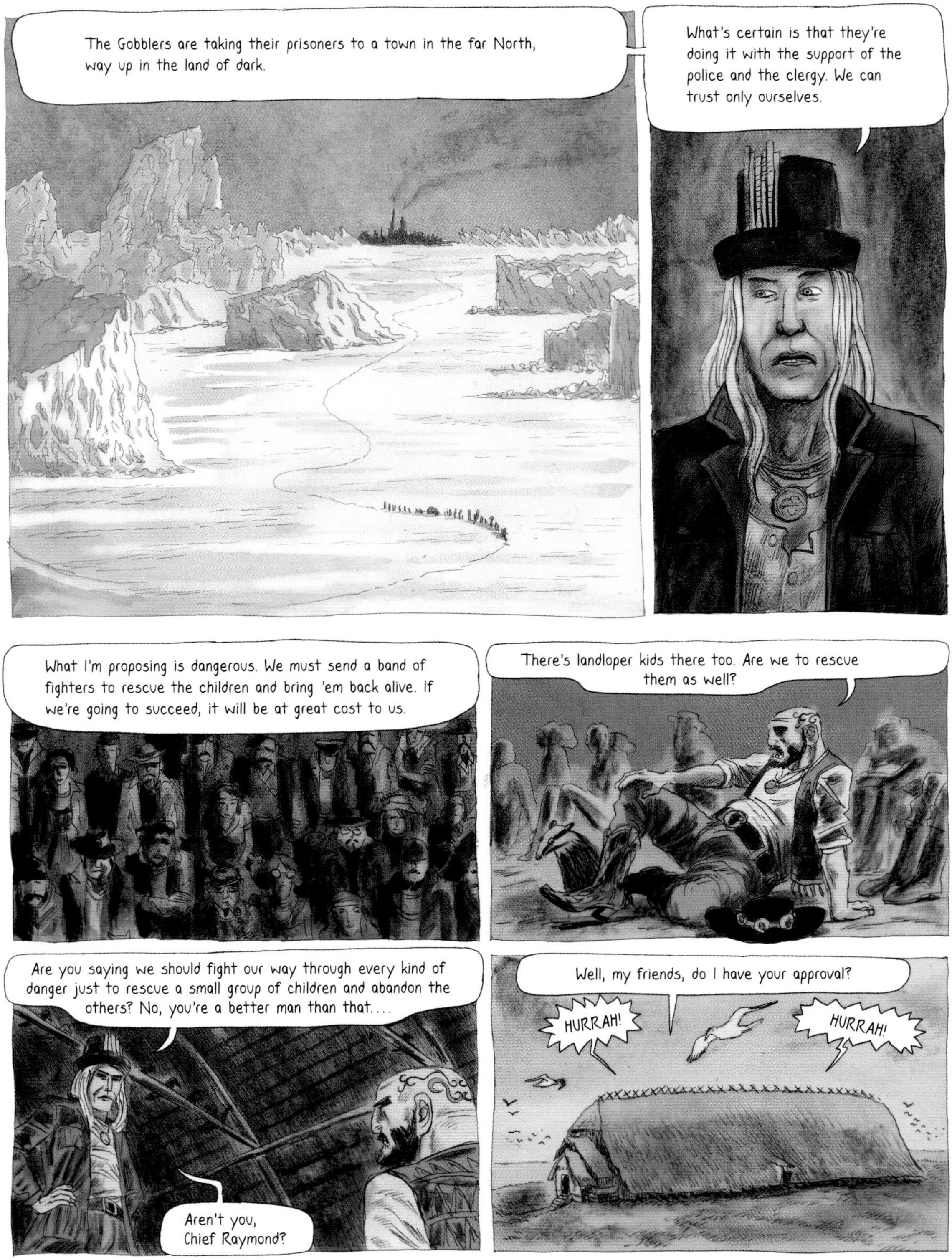

The Gobblers are taking their prisoners to a town in the far North, way up in the land of dark.
What's certain is that they're doing it with the support of the police and the clergy. We can trust only ourselves.
What I'm proposing is dangerous. We must send a band of fighters to rescue the children and bring 'em back alive. If we're going to succeed, it will be at great cost to us.
There's landloper kids there too. Are we to rescue them as well?
Are you saying we should fight our way through every kind of danger just to rescue a small group of children and abandon the others? No, you're a better man than that....
Aren't you, Chief Raymond?
Well, my friends, do I have your approval?
HURRAH!
HURRAH!

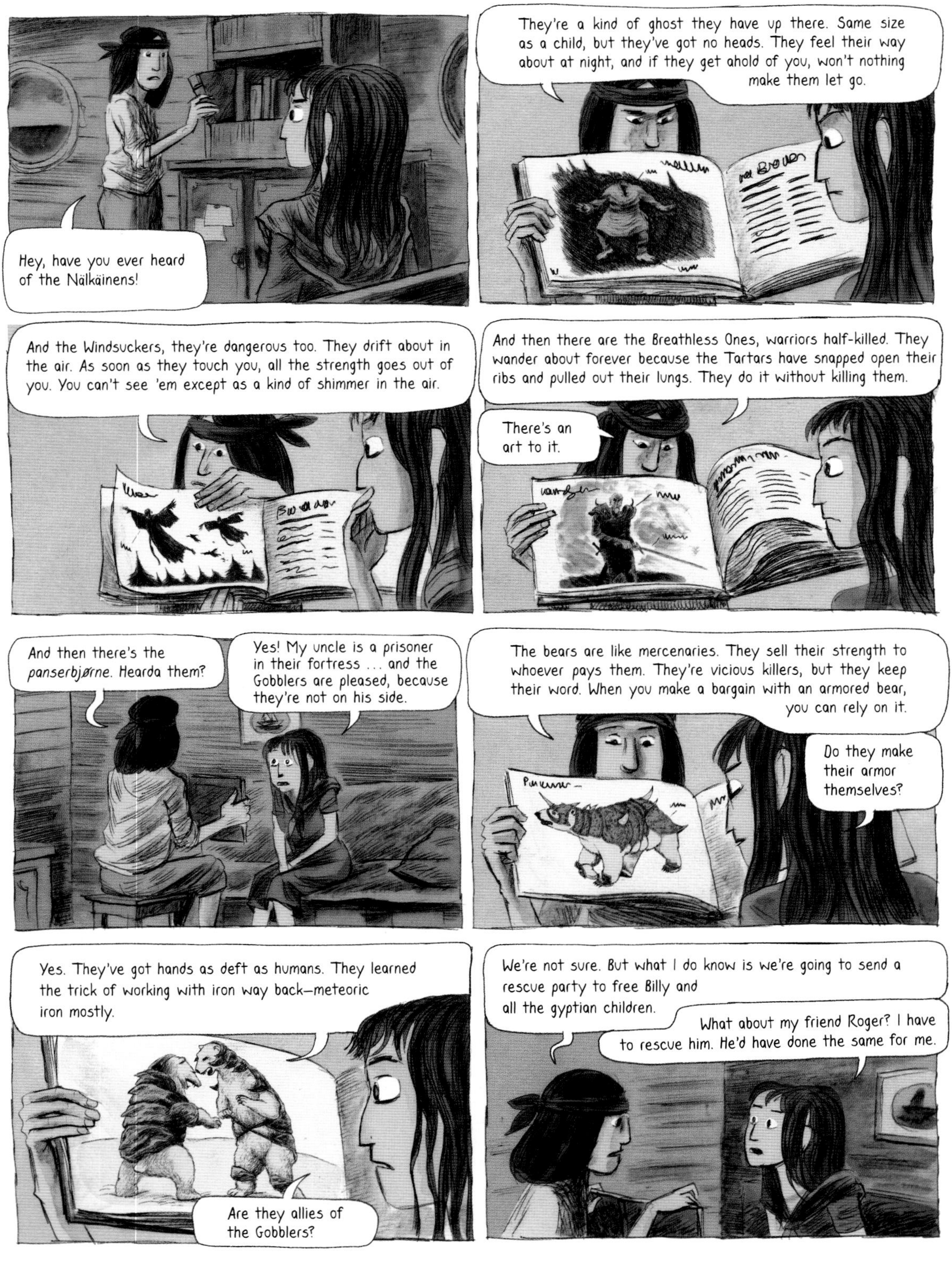
Hey, have you ever heard of the Nälkäinens!
They're a kind of ghost they have up there. Same size as a child, but they've got no heads. They feel their way about at night, and if they get ahold of you, won't nothing make them let go.
And the Windsuckers, they're dangerous too. They drift about in the air. As soon as they touch you, all the strength goes out of you. You can't see 'em except as a kind of shimmer in the air.
And then there are the Breathless Ones, warriors half-killed. They wander about forever because the Tartars have snapped open their ribs and pulled out their lungs. They do it without killing them.
There's an art to it.
And then there's the *panserbjørne*. Hearda them?
Yes! My uncle is a prisoner in their fortress ... and the Gobblers are pleased, because they're not on his side.
The bears are like mercenaries. They sell their strength to whoever pays them. They're vicious killers, but they keep their word. When you make a bargain with an armored bear, you can rely on it.
Do they make their armor themselves?
Yes. They've got hands as deft as humans. They learned the trick of working with iron way back—meteoric iron mostly.
Are they allies of the Gobblers?
We're not sure. But what I do know is we're going to send a rescue party to free Billy and all the gyptian children.
What about my friend Roger? I have to rescue him. He'd have done the same for me.

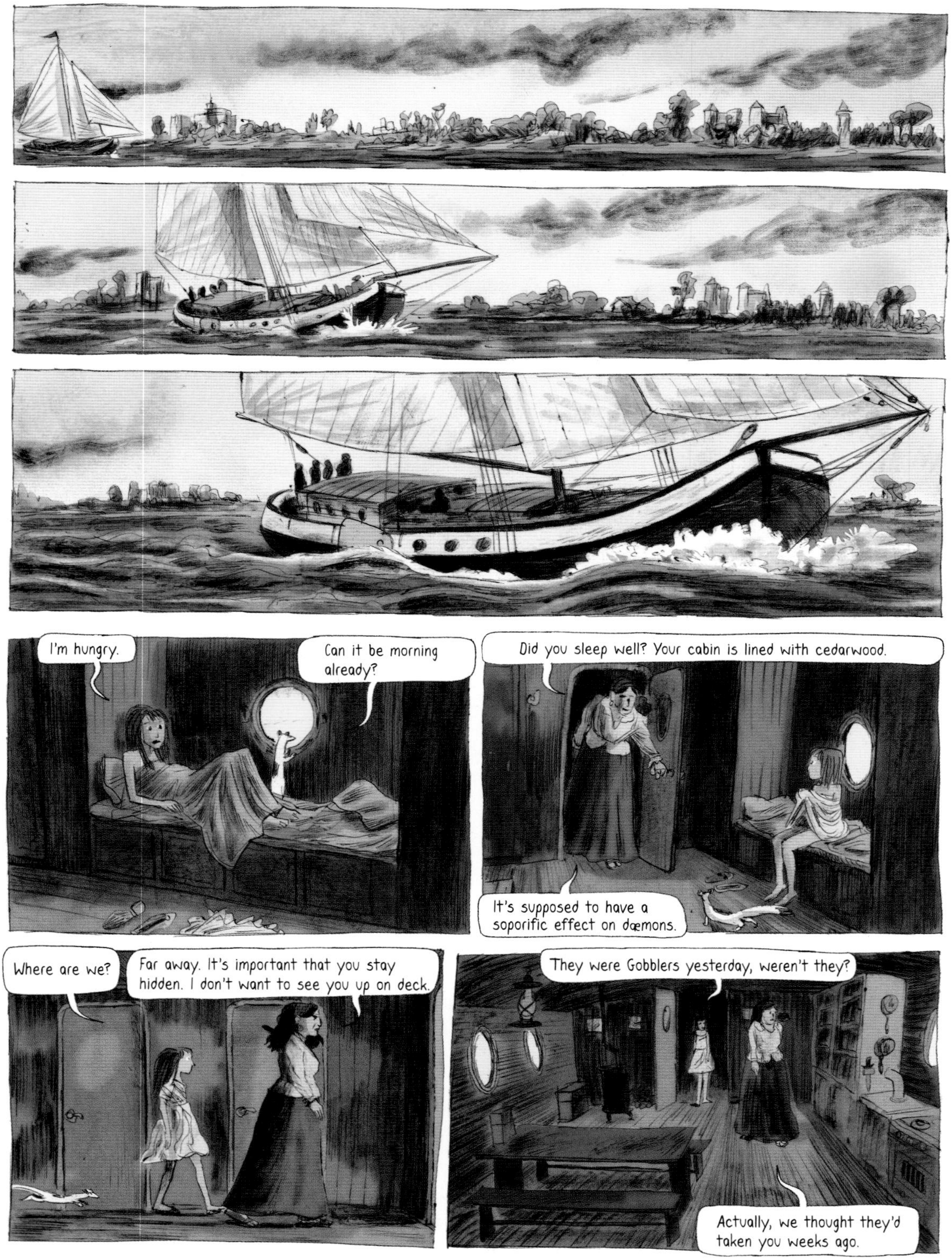
I'm hungry.
Can it be morning already?
Did you sleep well? Your cabin is lined with cedarwood.
It's supposed to have a soporific effect on dæmons.
Where are we?
Far away. It's important that you stay hidden. I don't want to see you up on deck.
They were Gobblers yesterday, weren't they?
Actually, we thought they'd taken you weeks ago.

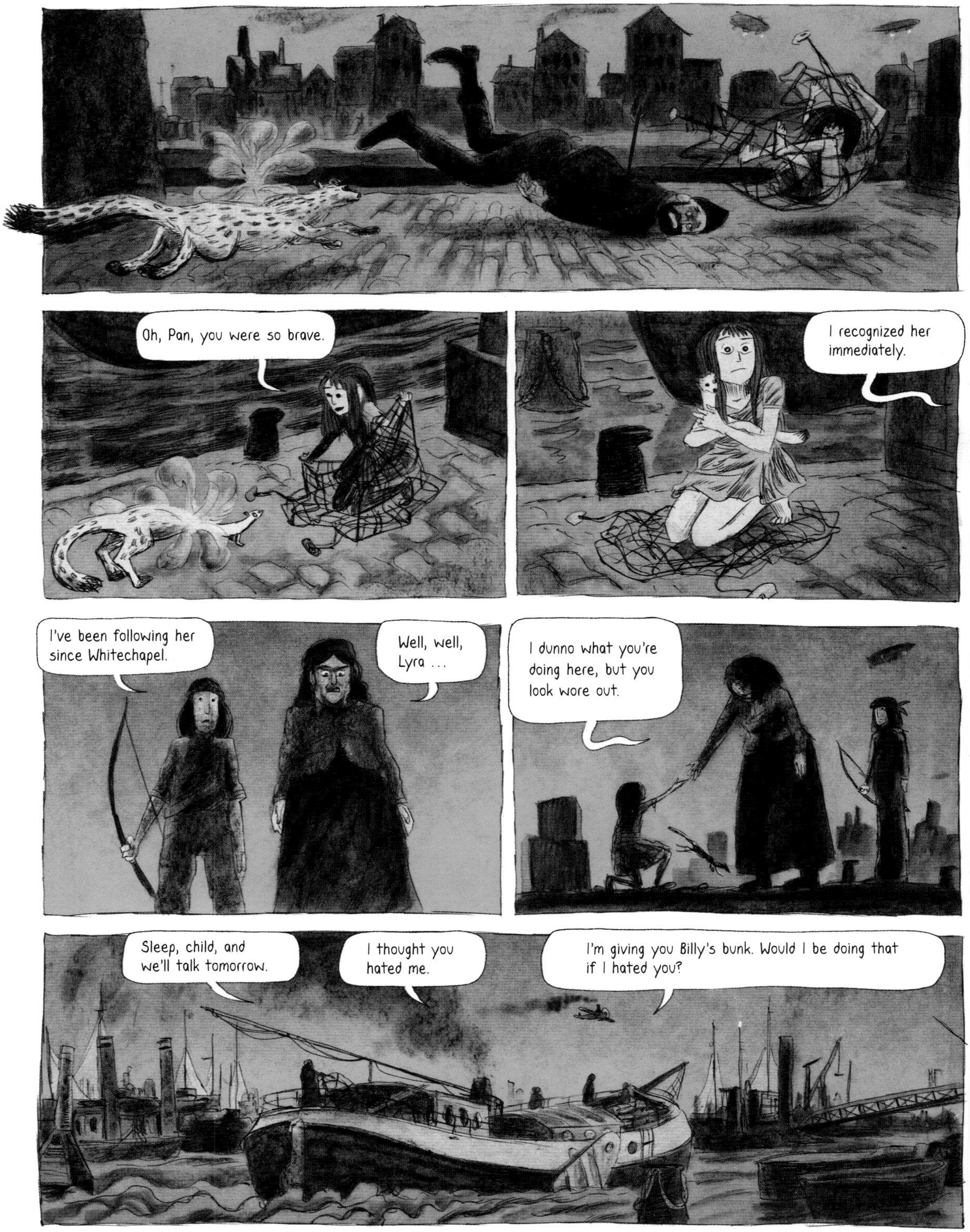
Oh, Pan, you were so brave.
I recognized her immediately.
I've been following her since Whitechapel.
Well, well, Lyra . . .
I dunno what you're doing here, but you look wore out.
Sleep, child, and we'll talk tomorrow.
I thought you hated me.
I'm giving you Billy's bunk. Would I be doing that if I hated you?

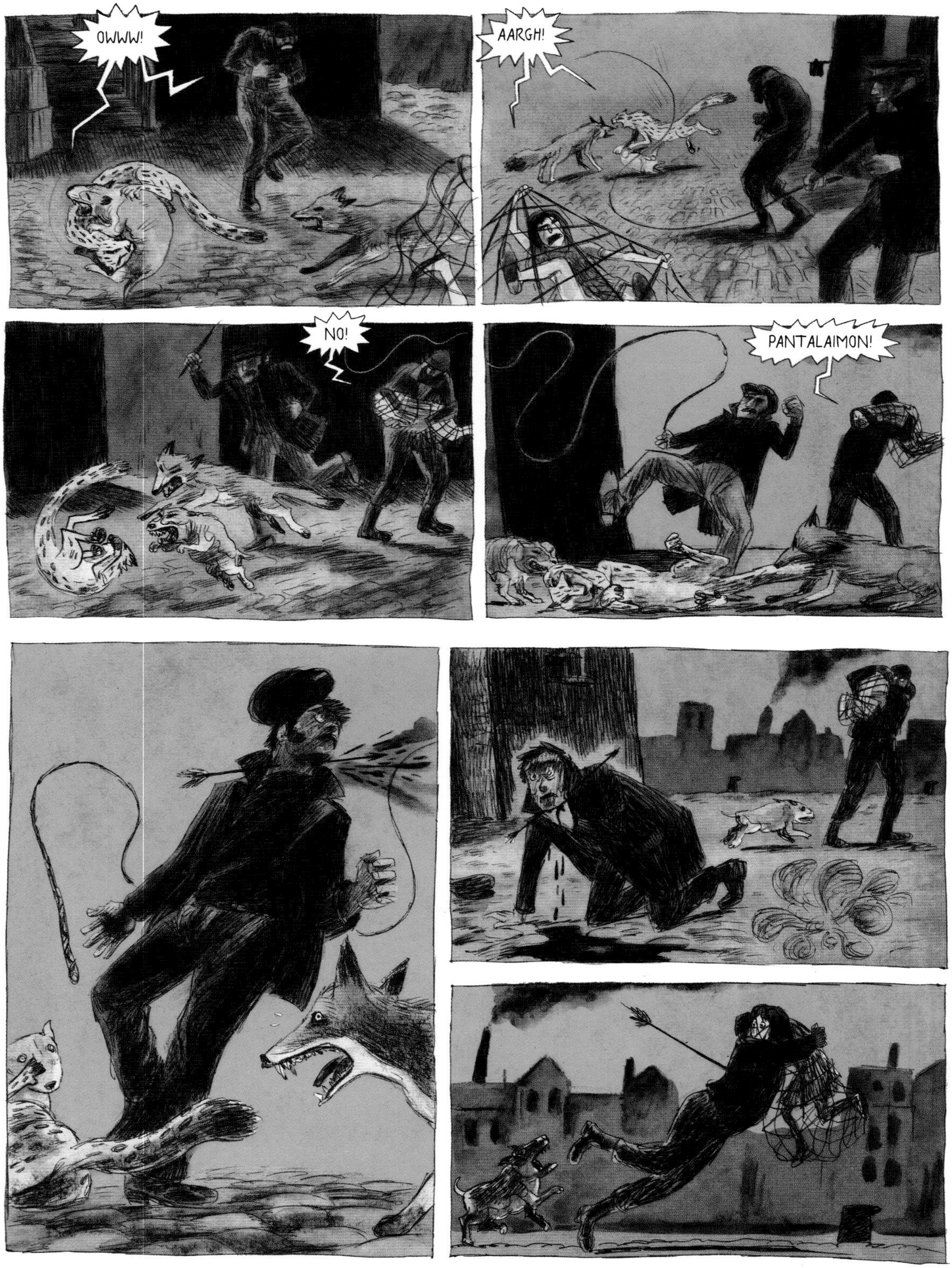
OWWW!
AARGH!
NO!
PANTALAIMON!

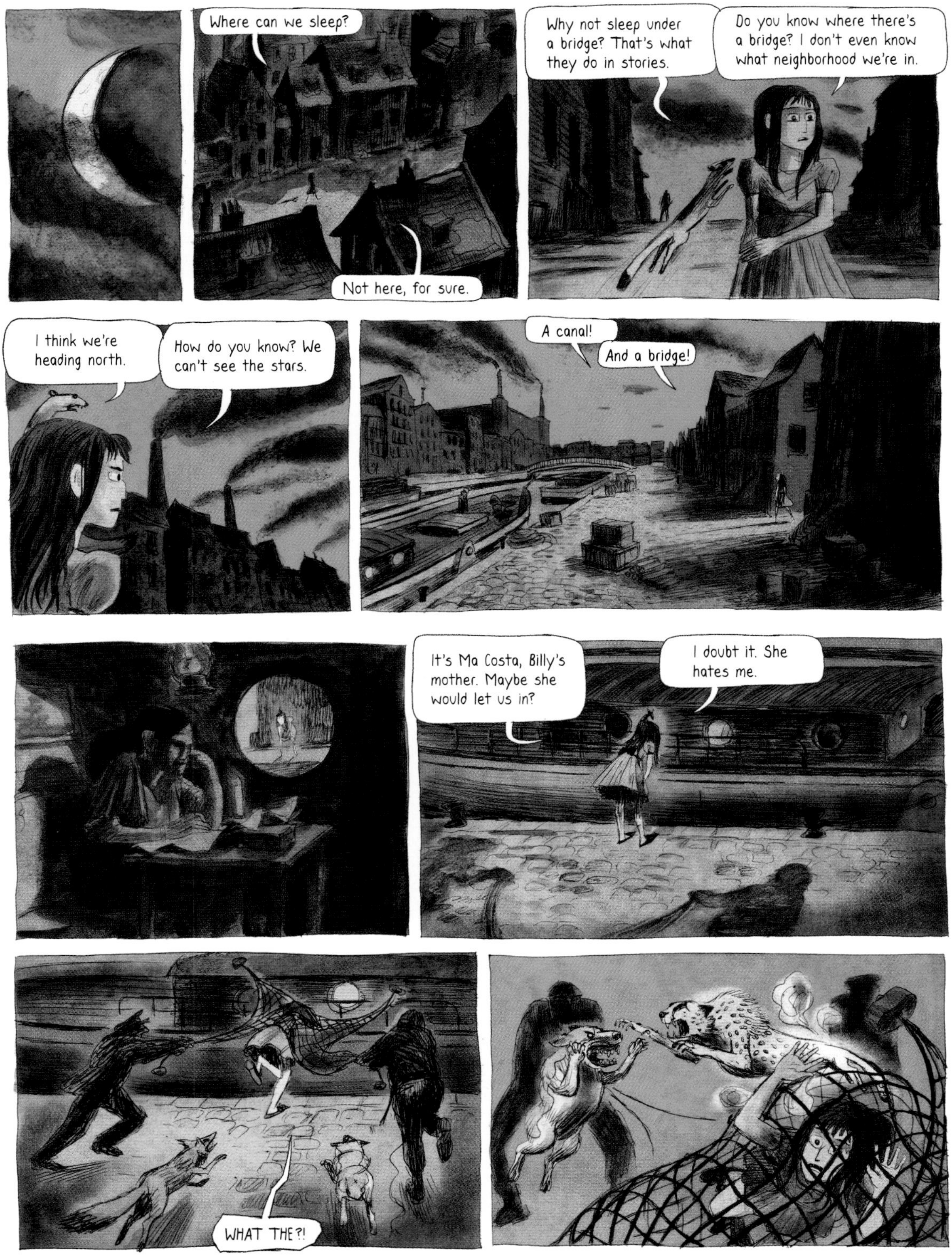
Where can we sleep?
Not here, for sure.
Why not sleep under a bridge? That's what they do in stories.
Do you know where there's a bridge? I don't even know what neighborhood we're in.
I think we're heading north.
How do you know? We can't see the stars.
A canal!
And a bridge!
It's Ma Costa, Billy's mother. Maybe she would let us in?
I doubt it. She hates me.
WHAT THE?!

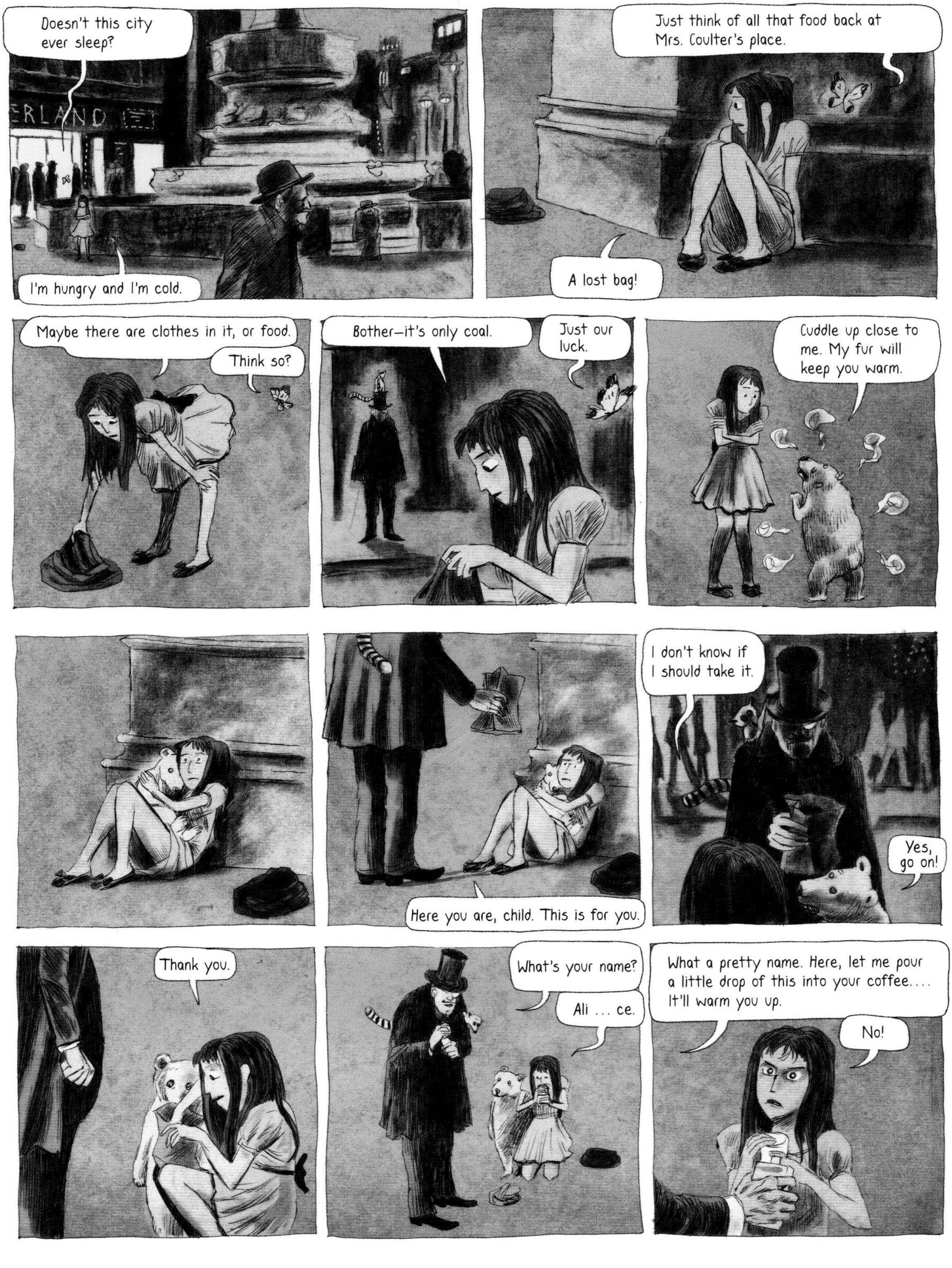
Doesn't this city ever sleep?
I'm hungry and I'm cold.
Just think of all that food back at Mrs. Coulter's place.
A lost bag!
Maybe there are clothes in it, or food.
Think so?
Bother—it's only coal.
Just our luck.
Cuddle up close to me. My fur will keep you warm.
Here you are, child. This is for you.
I don't know if I should take it.
Yes, go on!
Thank you.
What's your name?
Ali ... ce.
What a pretty name. Here, let me pour a little drop of this into your coffee.... It'll warm you up.
No!

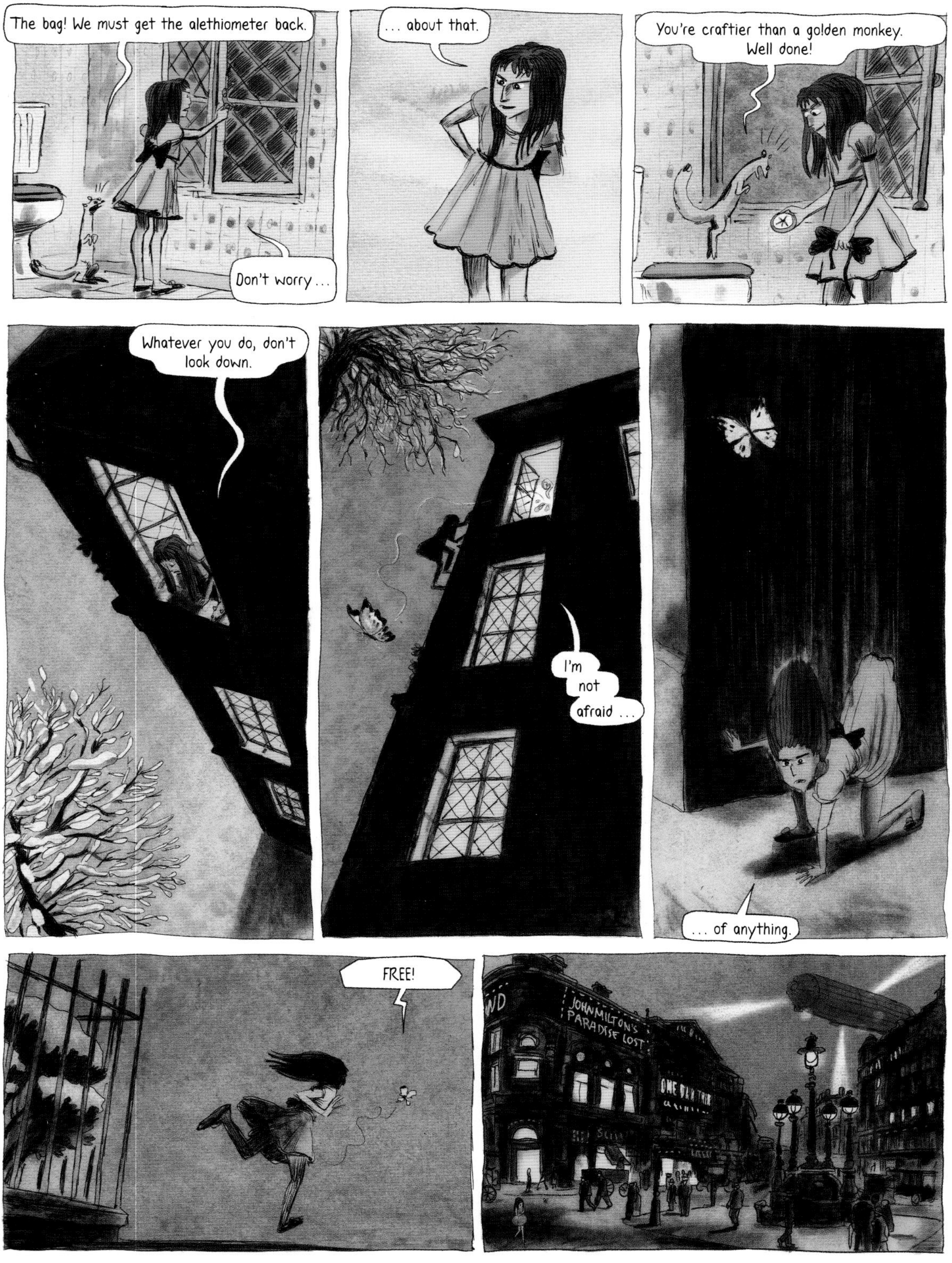
The bag! We must get the alethiometer back.
Don't worry . . .
. . . about that.
You're craftier than a golden monkey. Well done!
Whatever you do, don't look down.
I'm not afraid . . .
. . . of anything.
FREE!
JOHN MILTON'S PARADISE LOST

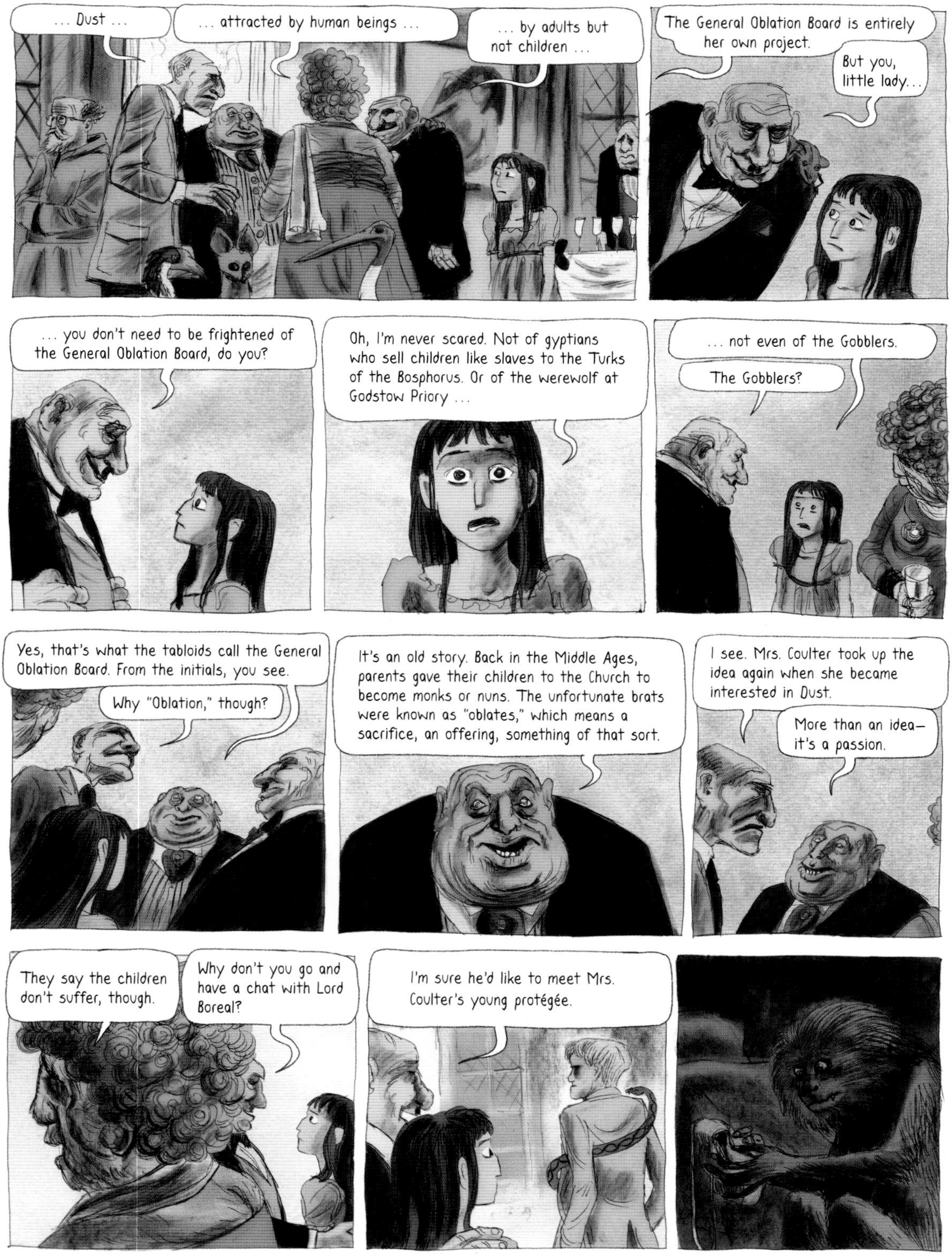
... Dust ...
... attracted by human beings ...
... by adults but not children ...
The General Oblation Board is entirely her own project.
But you, little lady...
... you don't need to be frightened of the General Oblation Board, do you?
Oh, I'm never scared. Not of gyptians who sell children like slaves to the Turks of the Bosphorus. Or of the werewolf at Godstow Priory ...
... not even of the Gobblers.
The Gobblers?
Yes, that's what the tabloids call the General Oblation Board. From the initials, you see.
Why "Oblation," though?
It's an old story. Back in the Middle Ages, parents gave their children to the Church to become monks or nuns. The unfortunate brats were known as "oblates," which means a sacrifice, an offering, something of that sort.
I see. Mrs. Coulter took up the idea again when she became interested in Dust.
More than an idea— it's a passion.
They say the children don't suffer, though.
Why don't you go and have a chat with Lord Boreal?
I'm sure he'd like to meet Mrs. Coulter's young protégée.

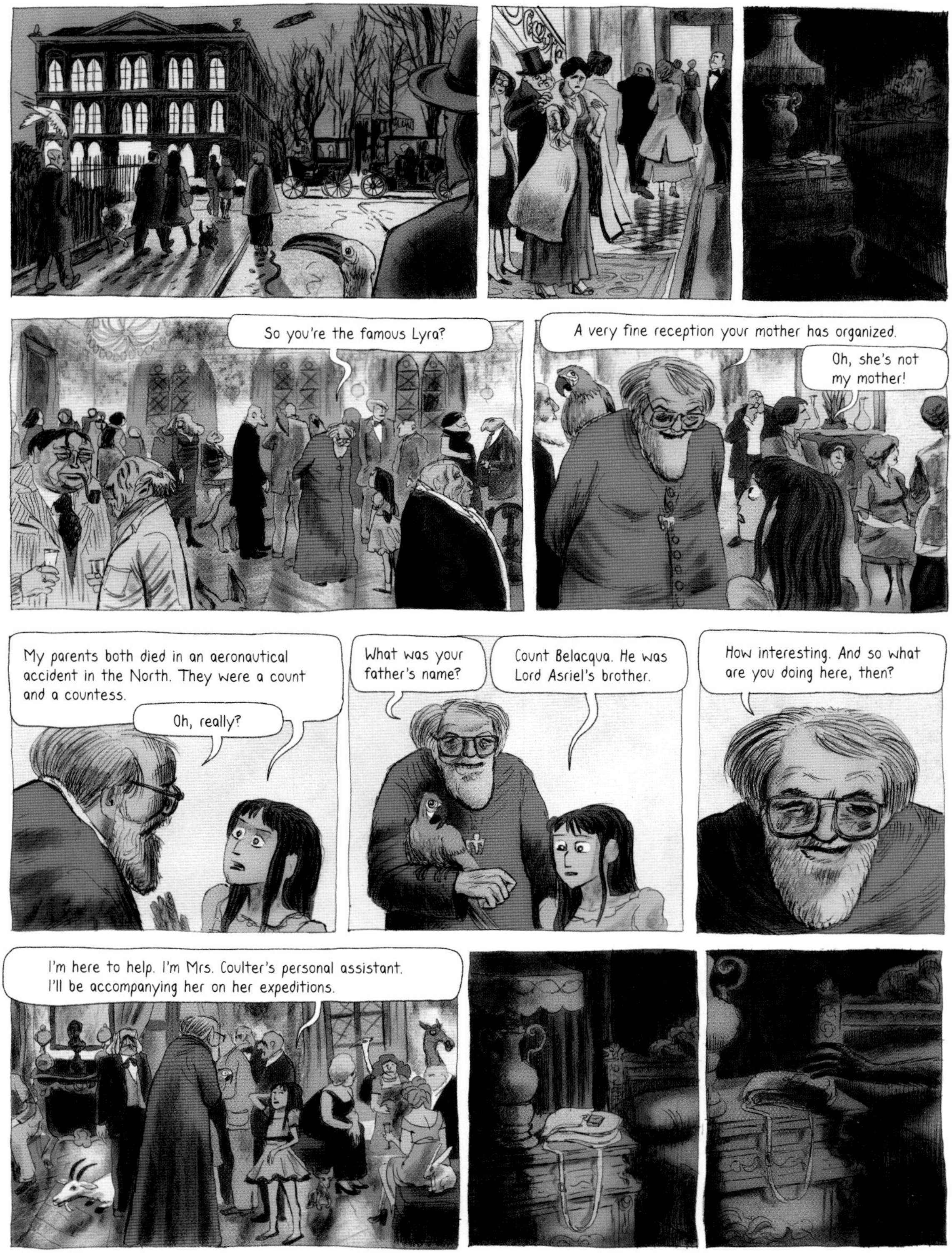
So you're the famous Lyra?
A very fine reception your mother has organized.
Oh, she's not my mother!
My parents both died in an aeronautical accident in the North. They were a count and a countess.
Oh, really?
What was your father's name?
Count Belacqua. He was Lord Asriel's brother.
How interesting. And so what are you doing here, then?
I'm here to help. I'm Mrs. Coulter's personal assistant. I'll be accompanying her on her expeditions.

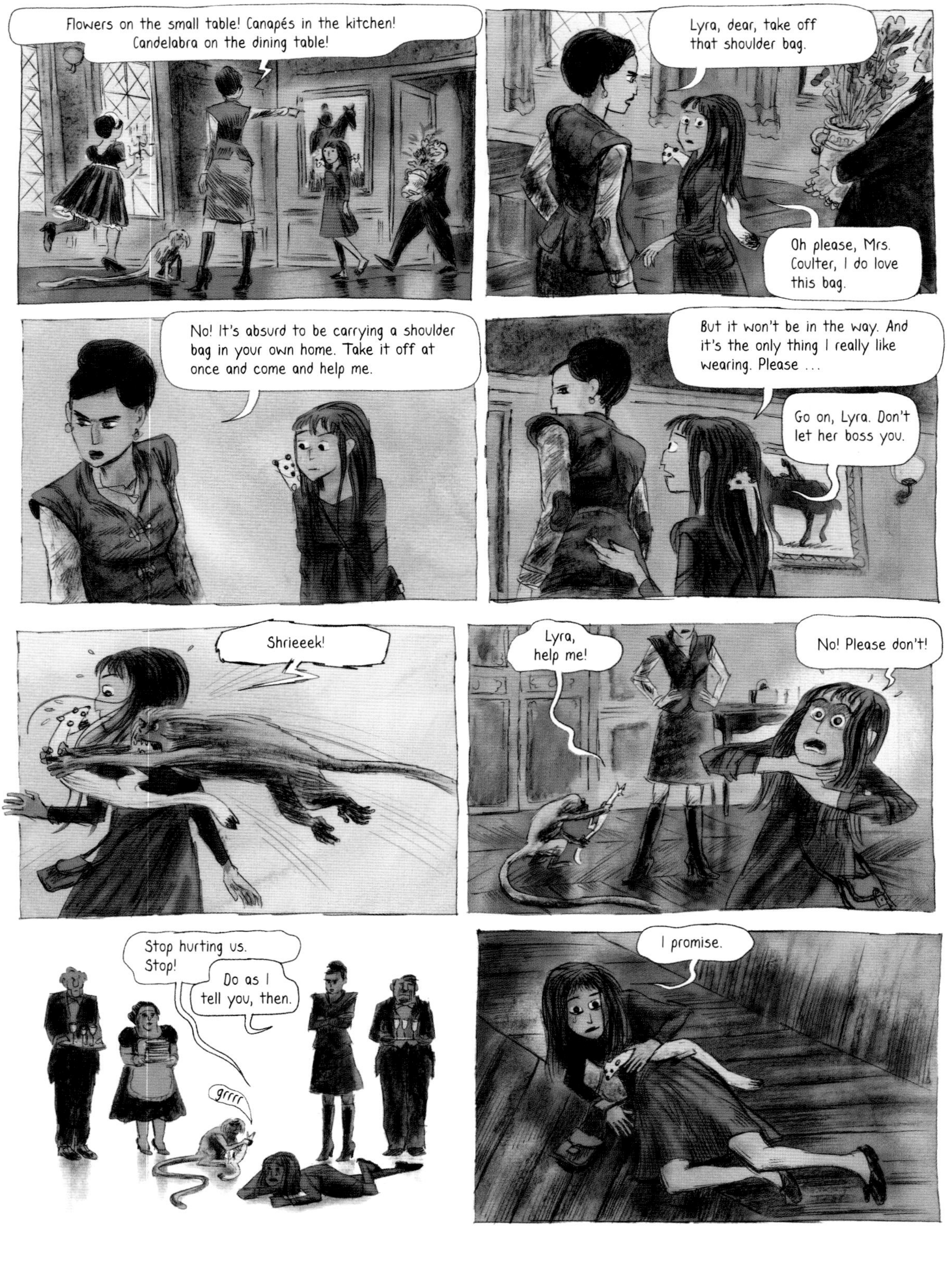

Flowers on the small table! Canapés in the kitchen! Candelabra on the dining table!
Lyra, dear, take off that shoulder bag.
Oh please, Mrs. Coulter, I do love this bag.
No! It's absurd to be carrying a shoulder bag in your own home. Take it off at once and come and help me.
But it won't be in the way. And it's the only thing I really like wearing. Please . . .
Go on, Lyra. Don't let her boss you.
Shrieeek!
Lyra, help me!
No! Please don't!
Stop hurting us. Stop!
Do as I tell you, then.
grrrr
I promise.

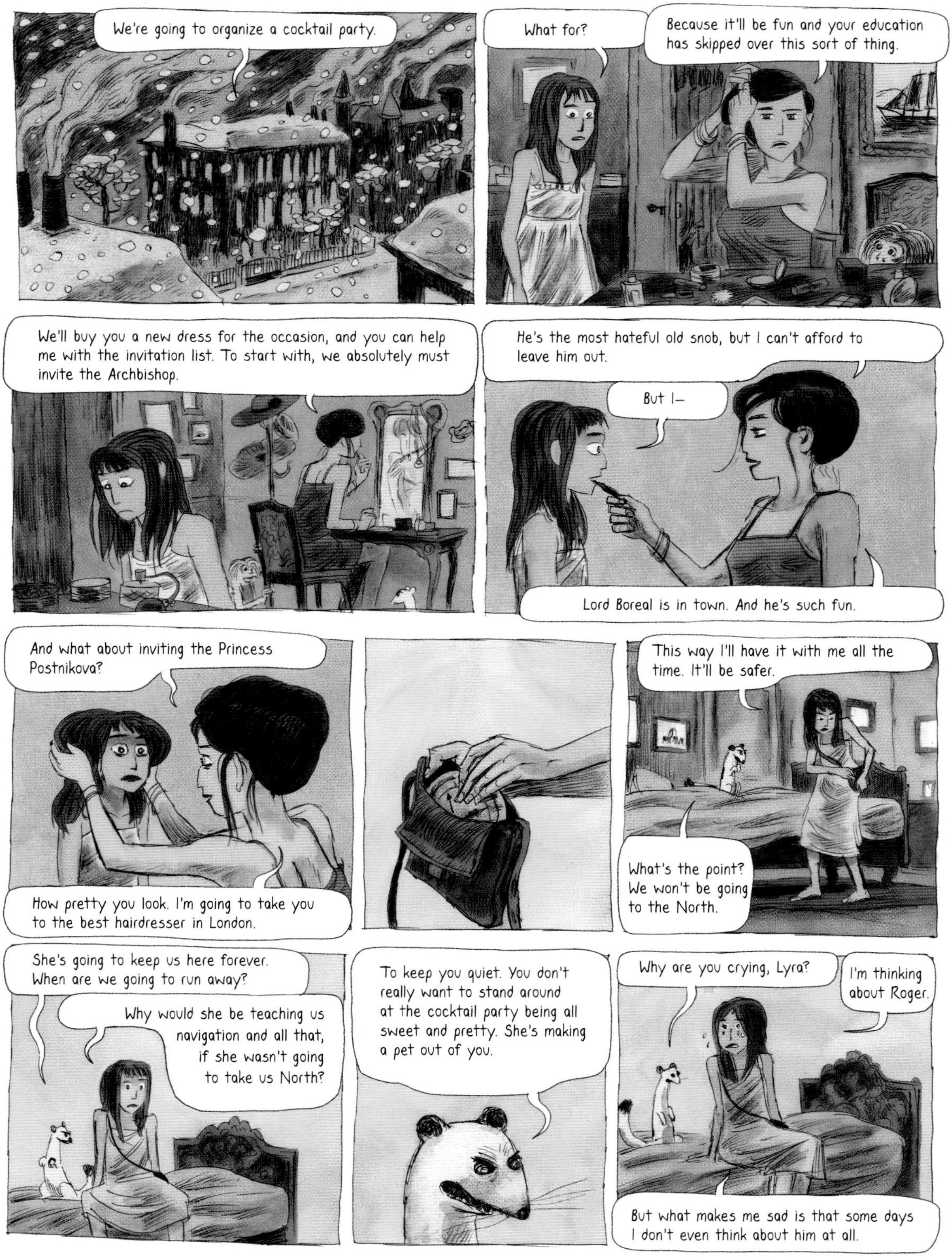
We're going to organize a cocktail party.
What for?
Because it'll be fun and your education has skipped over this sort of thing.
We'll buy you a new dress for the occasion, and you can help me with the invitation list. To start with, we absolutely must invite the Archbishop.
He's the most hateful old snob, but I can't afford to leave him out.
But I—
Lord Boreal is in town. And he's such fun.
And what about inviting the Princess Postnikova?
How pretty you look. I'm going to take you to the best hairdresser in London.
This way I'll have it with me all the time. It'll be safer.
What's the point? We won't be going to the North.
She's going to keep us here forever. When are we going to run away?
Why would she be teaching us navigation and all that, if she wasn't going to take us North?
To keep you quiet. You don't really want to stand around at the cocktail party being all sweet and pretty. She's making a pet out of you.
Why are you crying, Lyra?
I'm thinking about Roger.
But what makes me sad is that some days I don't even think about him at all.

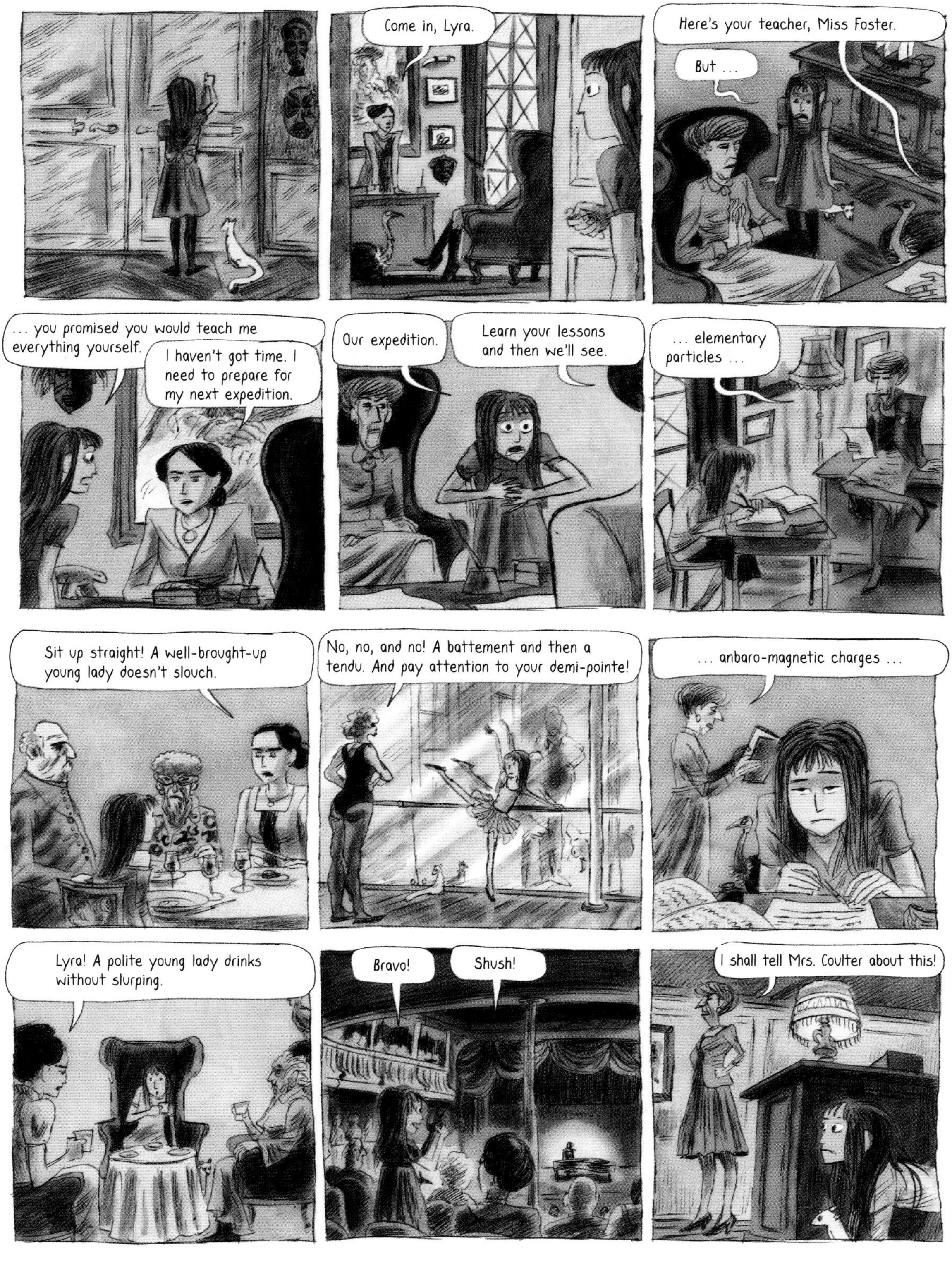
Come in, Lyra.
Here's your teacher, Miss Foster.
But . . .
. . . you promised you would teach me everything yourself.
I haven't got time. I need to prepare for my next expedition.
Our expedition.
Learn your lessons and then we'll see.
. . . elementary particles . . .
Sit up straight! A well-brought-up young lady doesn't slouch.
No, no, and no! A battement and then a tendu. And pay attention to your demi-pointe!
. . . anbaro-magnetic charges . . .
Lyra! A polite young lady drinks without slurping.
Bravo!
Shush!
I shall tell Mrs. Coulter about this!

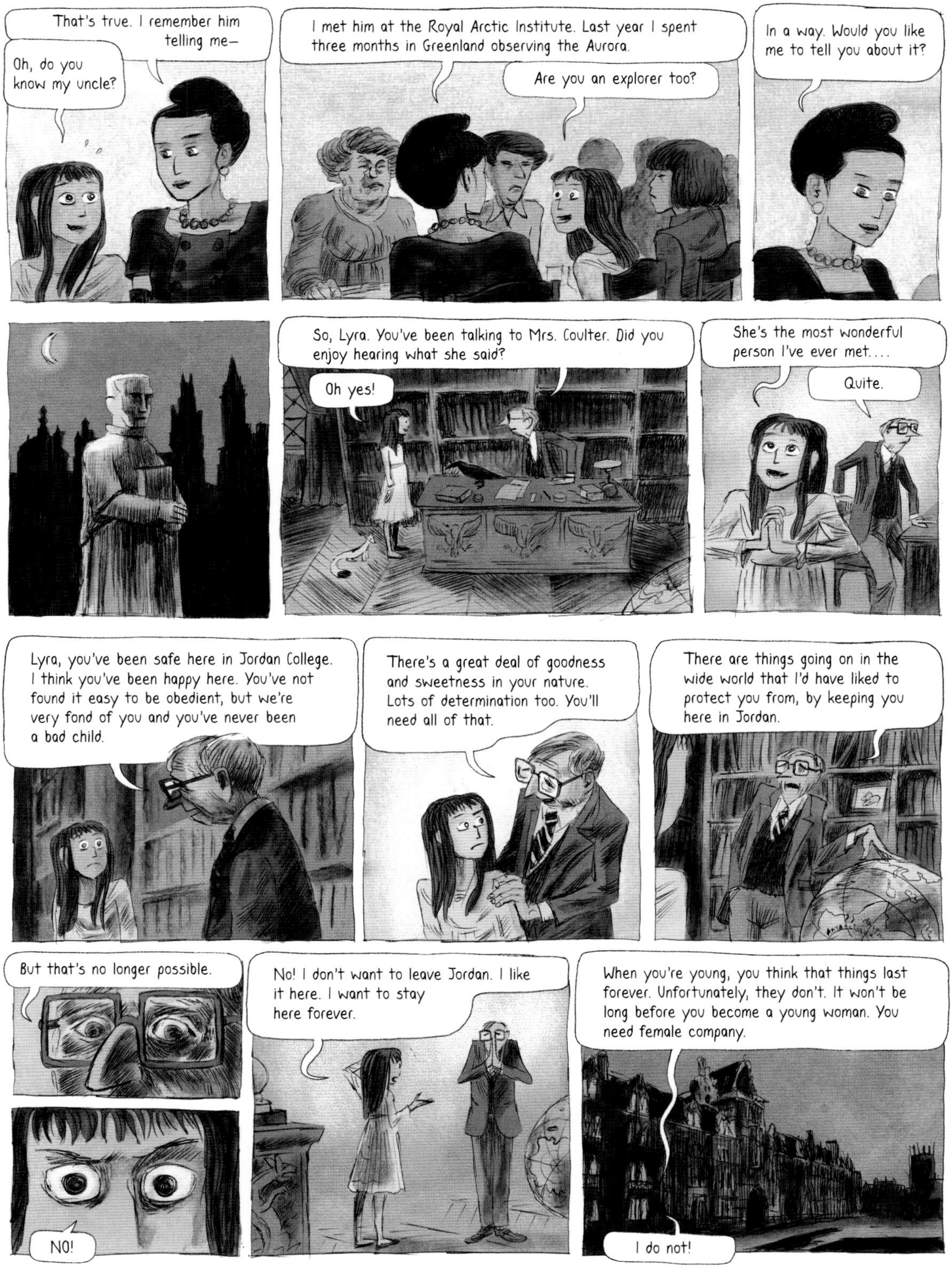
That's true. I remember him telling me—
Oh, do you know my uncle?
I met him at the Royal Arctic Institute. Last year I spent three months in Greenland observing the Aurora.
Are you an explorer too?
In a way. Would you like me to tell you about it?
So, Lyra. You've been talking to Mrs. Coulter. Did you enjoy hearing what she said?
Oh yes!
She's the most wonderful person I've ever met. . . .
Quite.
Lyra, you've been safe here in Jordan College. I think you've been happy here. You've not found it easy to be obedient, but we're very fond of you and you've never been a bad child.
There's a great deal of goodness and sweetness in your nature. Lots of determination too. You'll need all of that.
There are things going on in the wide world that I'd have liked to protect you from, by keeping you here in Jordan.
But that's no longer possible.
NO!
No! I don't want to leave Jordan. I like it here. I want to stay here forever.
When you're young, you think that things last forever. Unfortunately, they don't. It won't be long before you become a young woman. You need female company.
I do not!

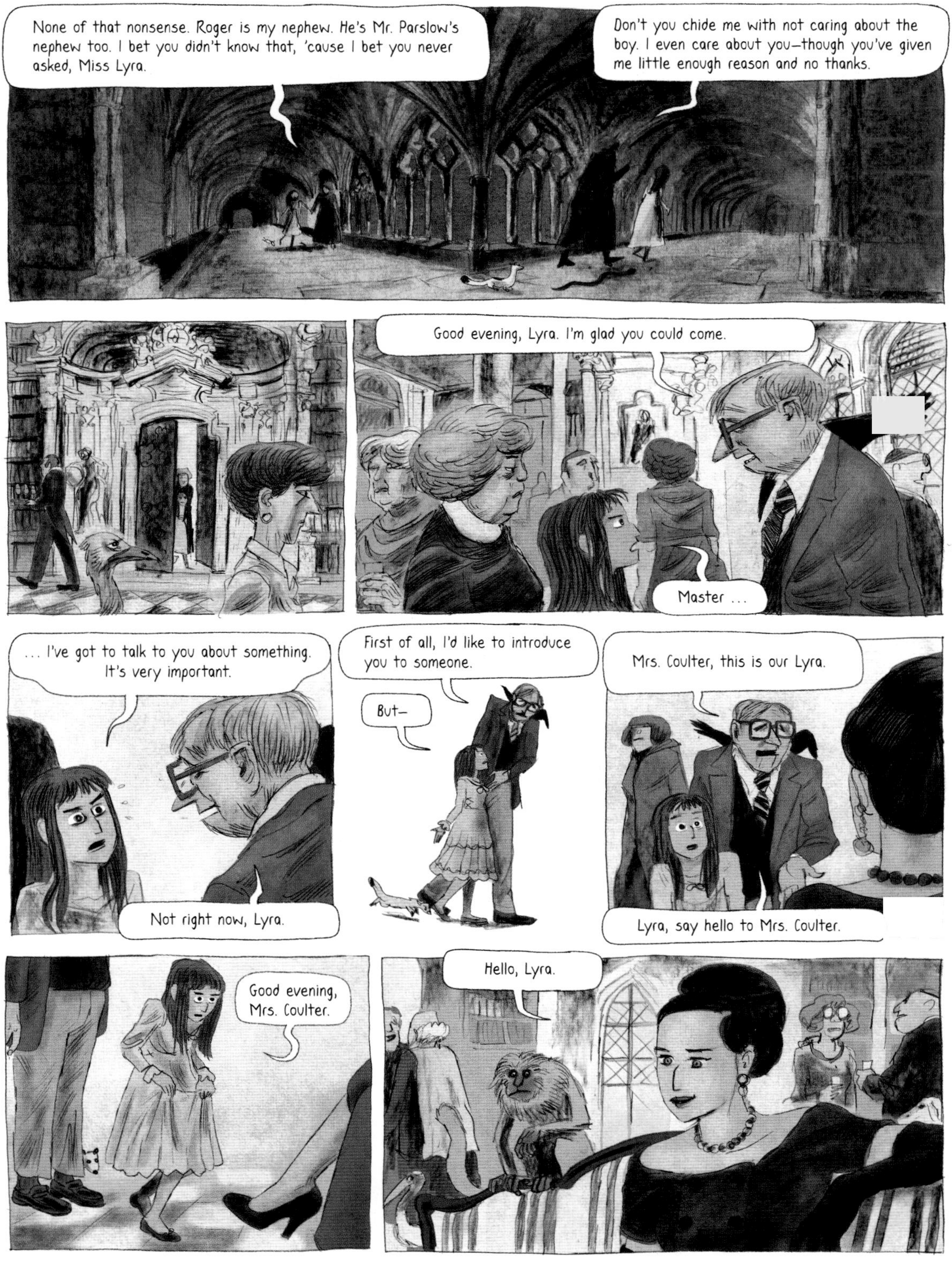
None of that nonsense. Roger is my nephew. He's Mr. Parslow's nephew too. I bet you didn't know that, 'cause I bet you never asked, Miss Lyra.
Don't you chide me with not caring about the boy. I even care about you—though you've given me little enough reason and no thanks.
Good evening, Lyra. I'm glad you could come.
Master . . .
. . . I've got to talk to you about something. It's very important.
Not right now, Lyra.
First of all, I'd like to introduce you to someone.
But—
Mrs. Coulter, this is our Lyra.
Lyra, say hello to Mrs. Coulter.
Good evening, Mrs. Coulter.
Hello, Lyra.

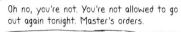

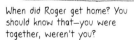

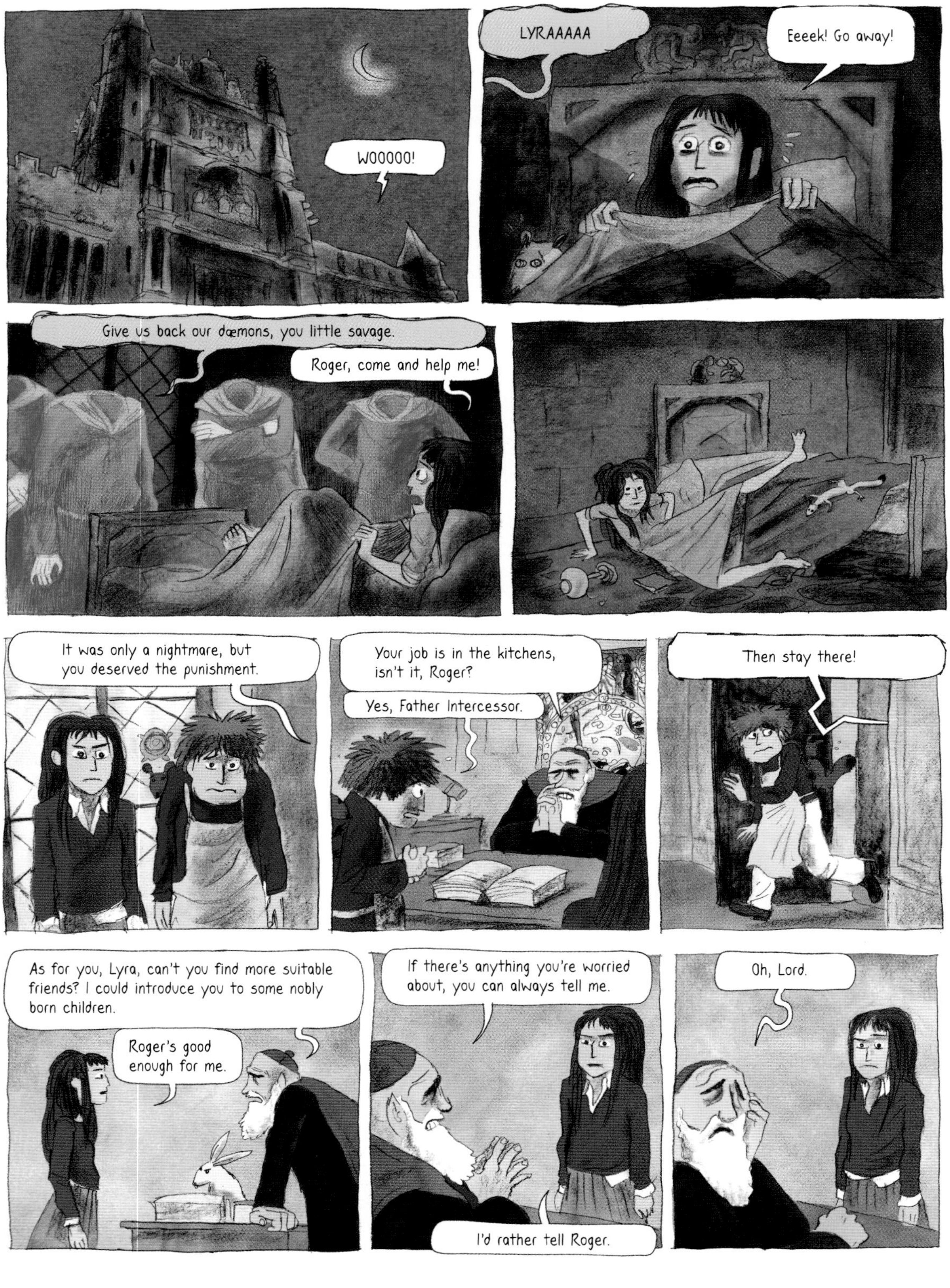
WOOOOO!
LYRAAAAA
Eeeek! Go away!
Give us back our dæmons, you little savage.
Roger, come and help me!
It was only a nightmare, but you deserved the punishment.
Your job is in the kitchens, isn't it, Roger?
Yes, Father Intercessor.
Then stay there!
As for you, Lyra, can't you find more suitable friends? I could introduce you to some nobly born children.
Roger's good enough for me.
If there's anything you're worried about, you can always tell me.
I'd rather tell Roger.
Oh, Lord.

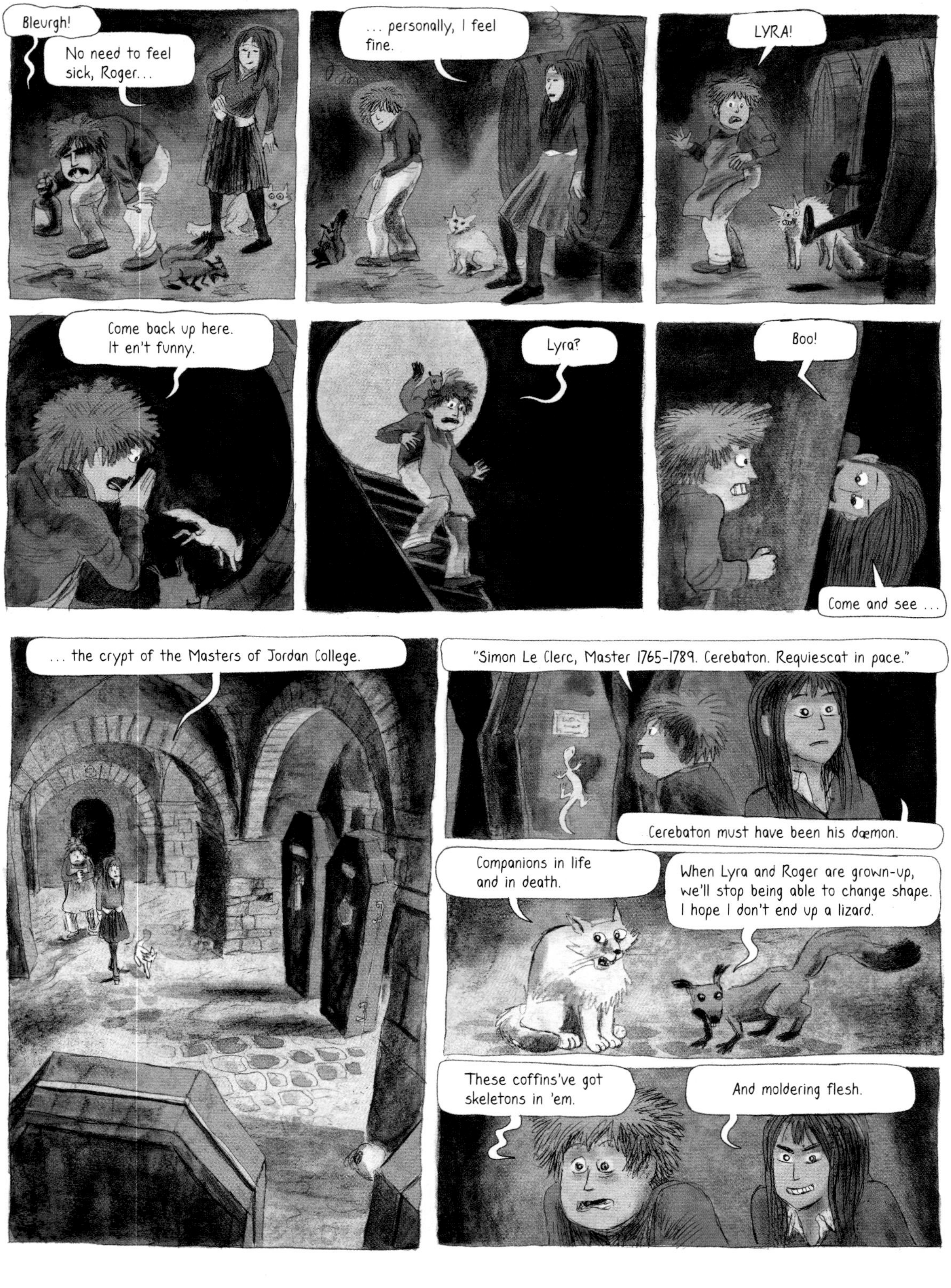
Bleurgh!
No need to feel sick, Roger...
... personally, I feel fine.
LYRA!
Come back up here. It en't funny.
Lyra?
Boo!
Come and see ...
... the crypt of the Masters of Jordan College.
"Simon Le Clerc, Master 1765-1789. Cerebaton. Requiescat in pace."
Cerebaton must have been his dæmon.
Companions in life and in death.
When Lyra and Roger are grown-up, we'll stop being able to change shape. I hope I don't end up a lizard.
These coffins've got skeletons in 'em.
And moldering flesh.

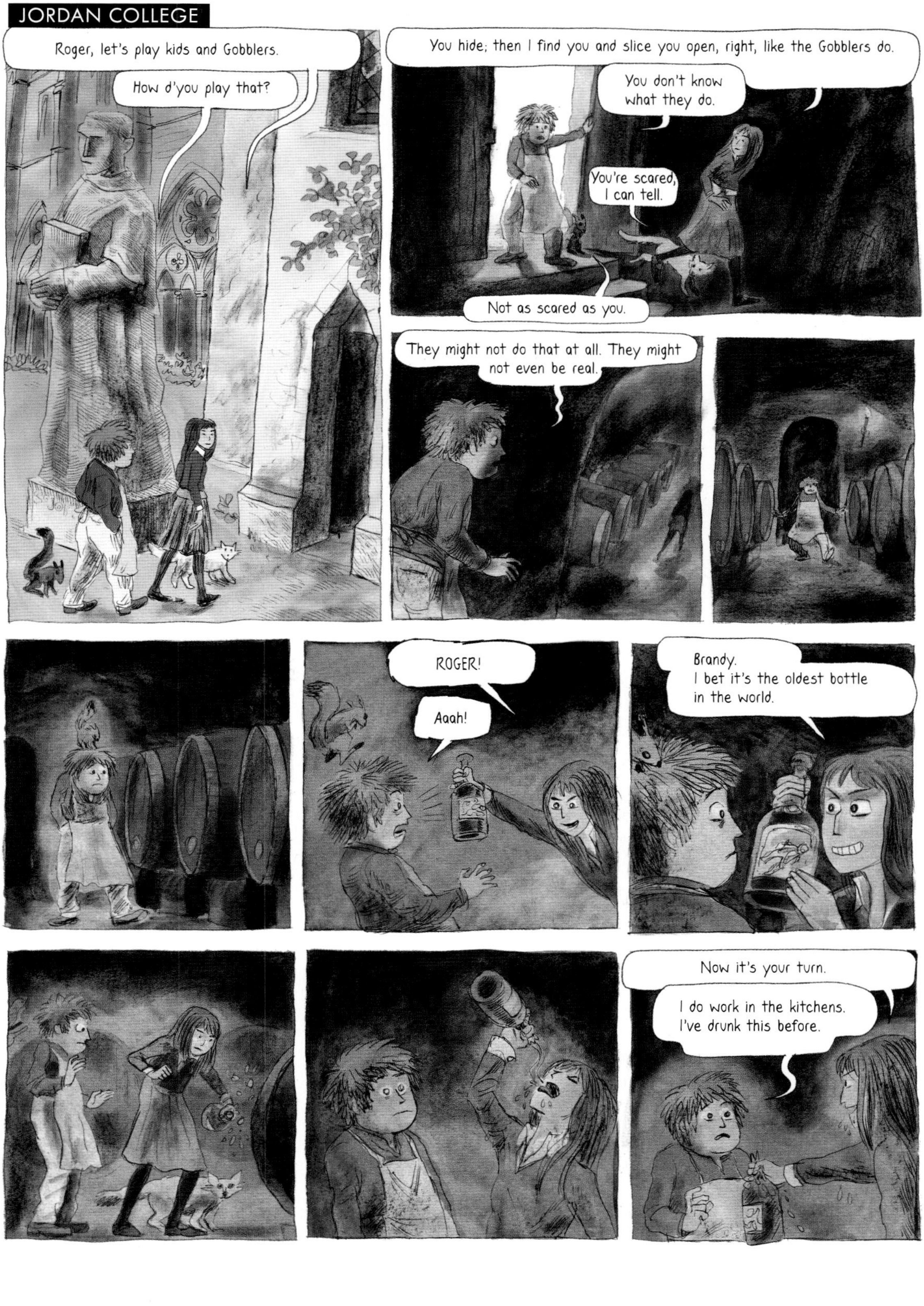
JORDAN COLLEGE
Roger, let's play kids and Gobblers.
How d'you play that?
You hide; then I find you and slice you open, right, like the Gobblers do.
You don't know what they do.
You're scared, I can tell.
Not as scared as you.
They might not do that at all. They might not even be real.
ROGER!
Aaah!
Brandy.
I bet it's the oldest bottle in the world.
Now it's your turn.
I do work in the kitchens.
I've drunk this before.

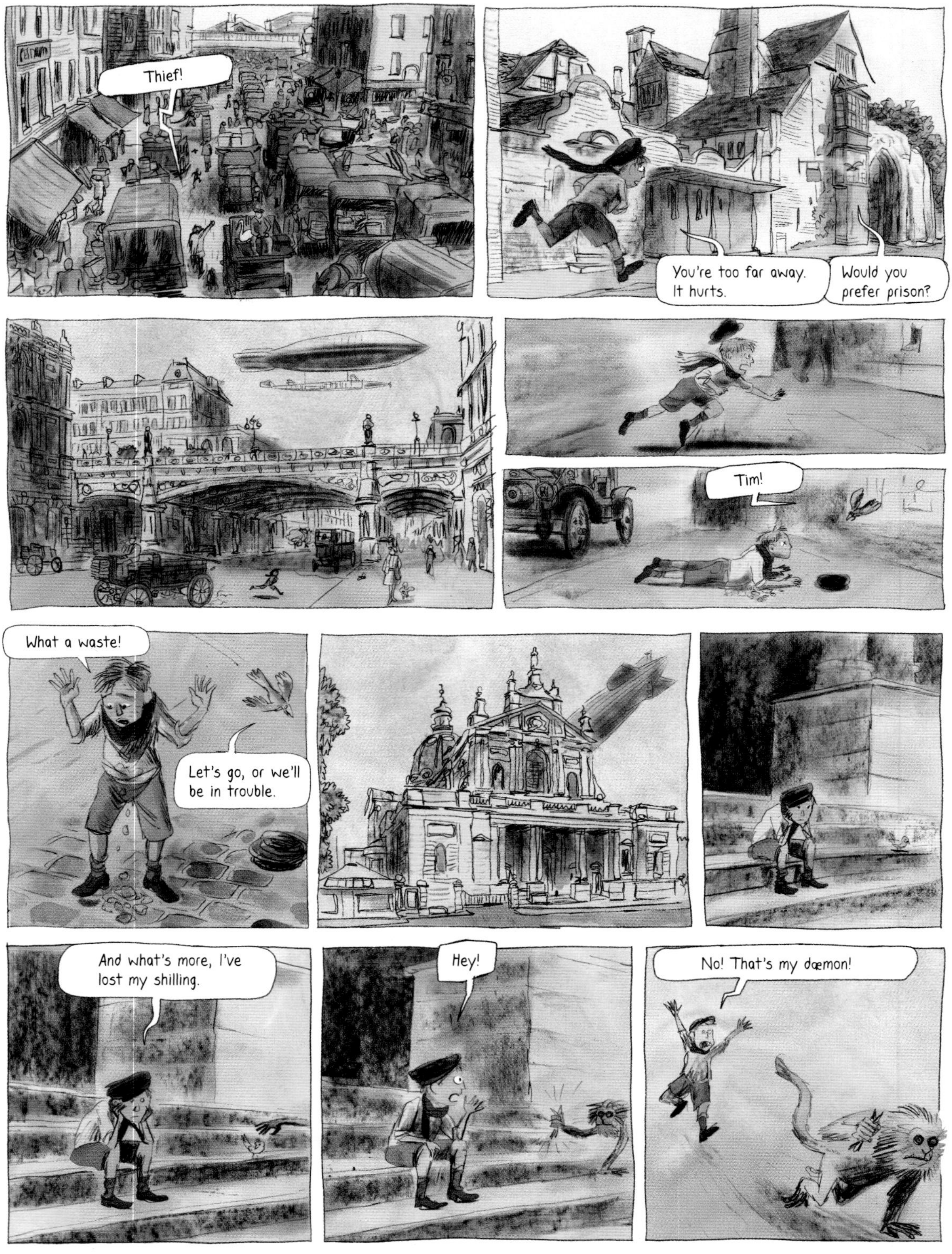
Thief!
You're too far away. It hurts.
Would you prefer prison?
Tim!
What a waste!
Let's go, or we'll be in trouble.
And what's more, I've lost my shilling.
Hey!
No! That's my dæmon!

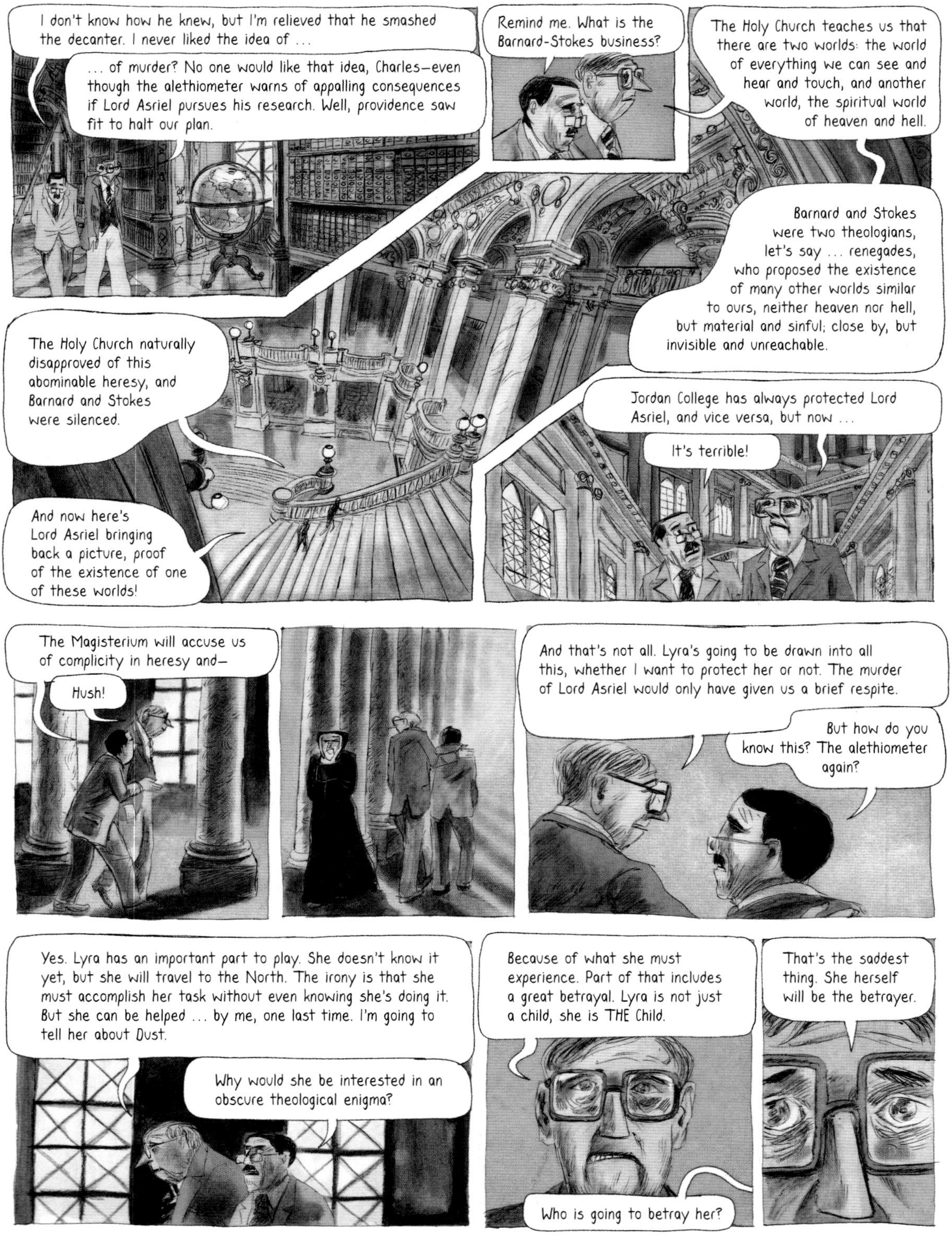
I don't know how he knew, but I'm relieved that he smashed the decanter. I never liked the idea of ...
... of murder? No one would like that idea, Charles—even though the alethiometer warns of appalling consequences if Lord Asriel pursues his research. Well, providence saw fit to halt our plan.
Remind me. What is the Barnard-Stokes business?
The Holy Church teaches us that there are two worlds: the world of everything we can see and hear and touch, and another world, the spiritual world of heaven and hell.
Barnard and Stokes were two theologians, let's say ... renegades, who proposed the existence of many other worlds similar to ours, neither heaven nor hell, but material and sinful; close by, but invisible and unreachable.
The Holy Church naturally disapproved of this abominable heresy, and Barnard and Stokes were silenced.
And now here's Lord Asriel bringing back a picture, proof of the existence of one of these worlds!
Jordan College has always protected Lord Asriel, and vice versa, but now ...
It's terrible!
The Magisterium will accuse us of complicity in heresy and—
Hush!
And that's not all. Lyra's going to be drawn into all this, whether I want to protect her or not. The murder of Lord Asriel would only have given us a brief respite.
But how do you know this? The alethiometer again?
Yes. Lyra has an important part to play. She doesn't know it yet, but she will travel to the North. The irony is that she must accomplish her task without even knowing she's doing it. But she can be helped ... by me, one last time. I'm going to tell her about Dust.
Why would she be interested in an obscure theological enigma?
Because of what she must experience. Part of that includes a great betrayal. Lyra is not just a child, she is THE Child.
Who is going to betray her?
That's the saddest thing. She herself will be the betrayer.

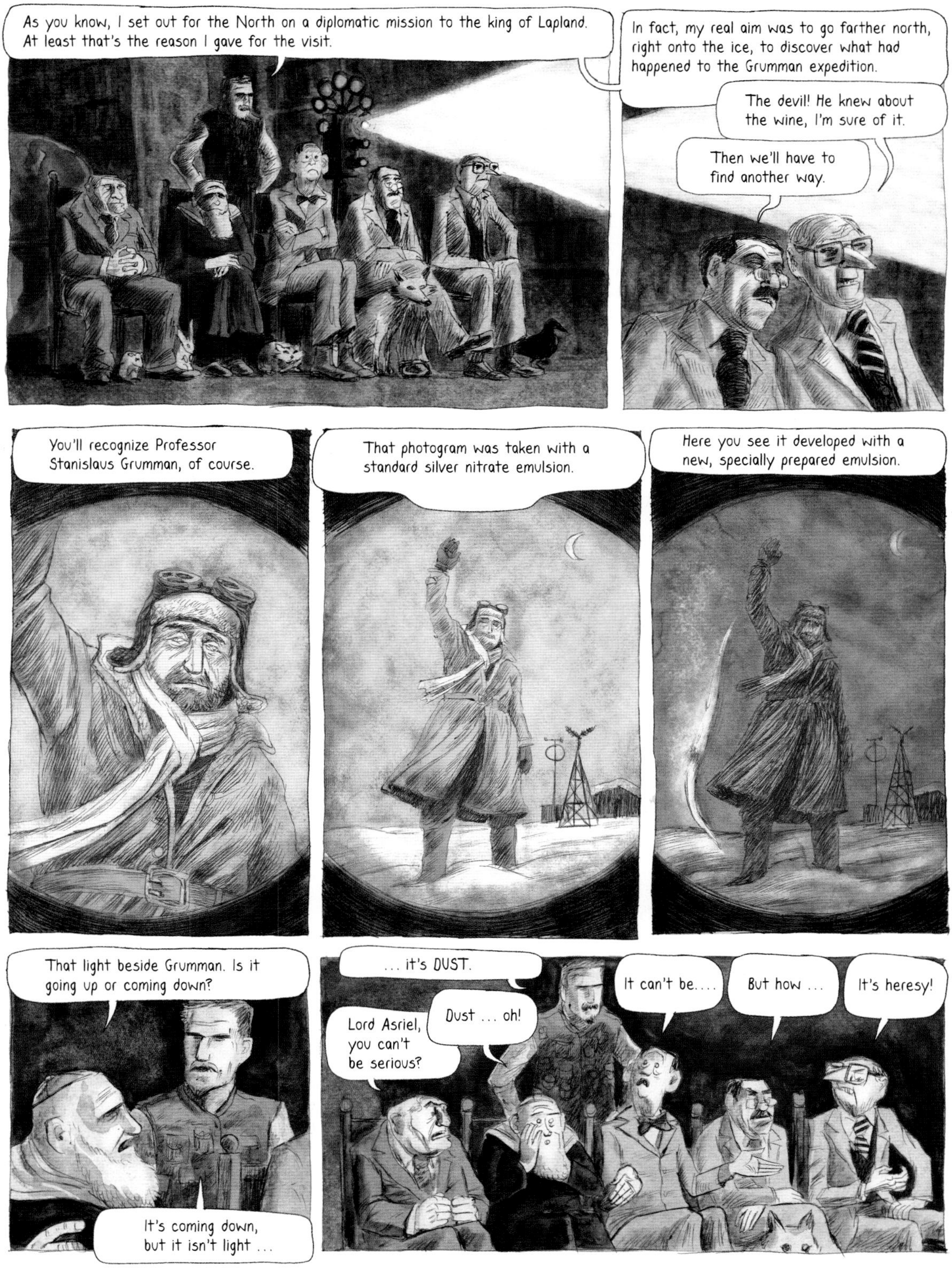
As you know, I set out for the North on a diplomatic mission to the king of Lapland. At least that's the reason I gave for the visit.
In fact, my real aim was to go farther north, right onto the ice, to discover what had happened to the Grumman expedition.
The devil! He knew about the wine, I'm sure of it.
Then we'll have to find another way.
You'll recognize Professor Stanislaus Grumman, of course.
That photogram was taken with a standard silver nitrate emulsion.
Here you see it developed with a new, specially prepared emulsion.
That light beside Grumman. Is it going up or coming down?
It's coming down, but it isn't light . . .
. . . it's DUST.
Lord Asriel, you can't be serious?
Dust . . . oh!
It can't be. . . .
But how . . .
It's heresy!

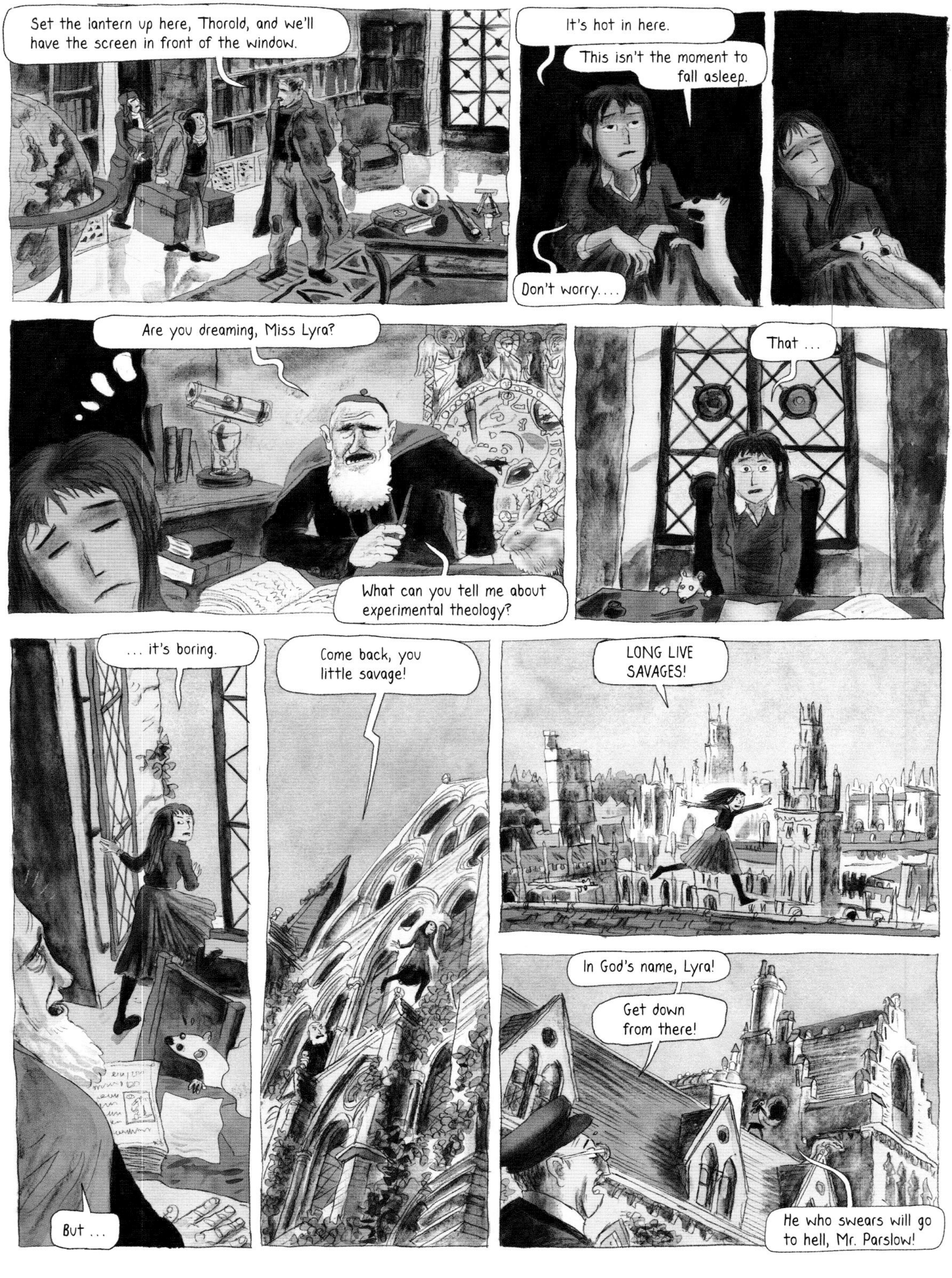
Set the lantern up here, Thorold, and we'll have the screen in front of the window.
It's hot in here.
This isn't the moment to fall asleep.
Don't worry. . . .
Are you dreaming, Miss Lyra?
What can you tell me about experimental theology?
That . . .
. . . it's boring.
But . . .
Come back, you little savage!
LONG LIVE SAVAGES!
In God's name, Lyra!
Get down from there!
He who swears will go to hell, Mr. Parslow!

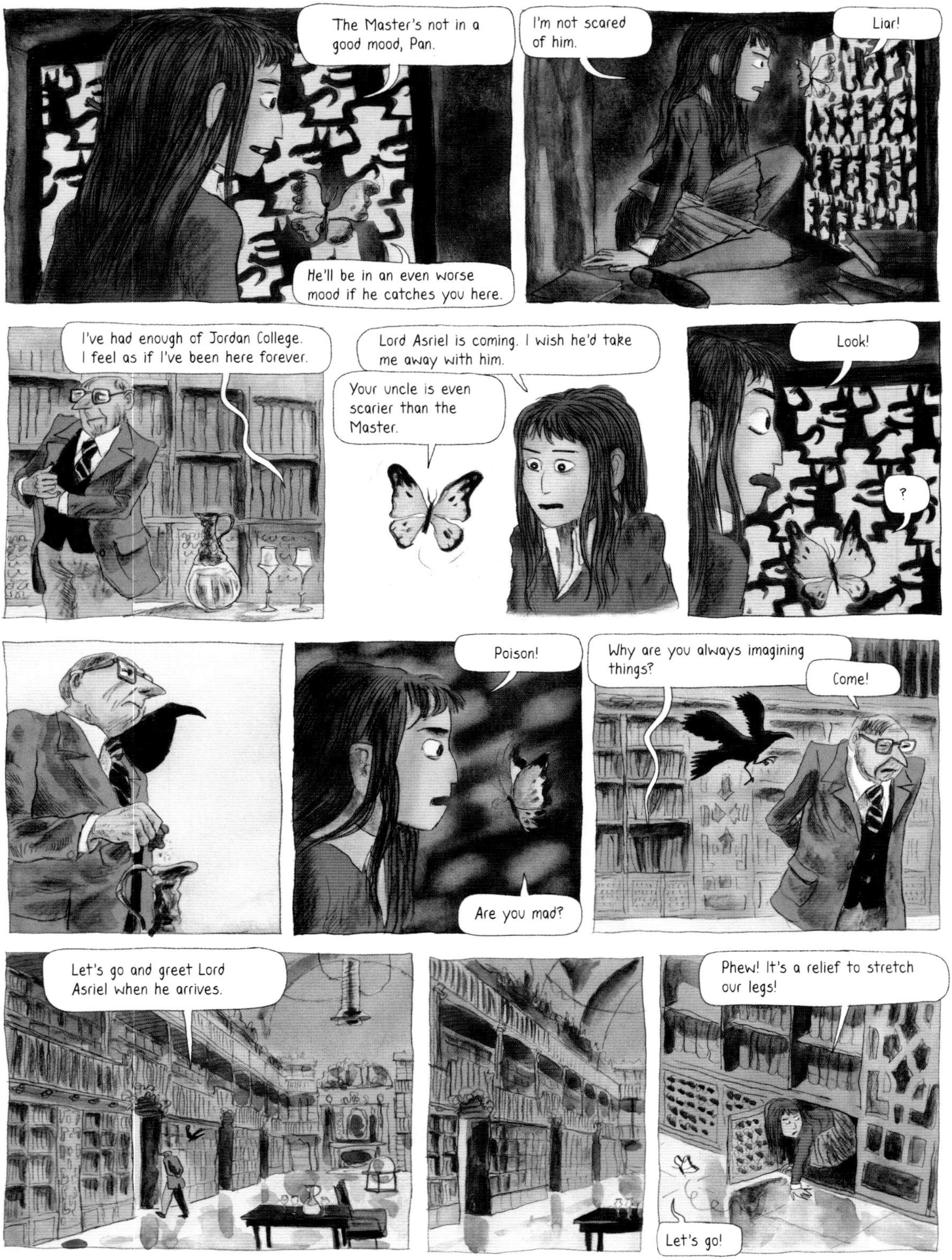
The Master's not in a good mood, Pan.
He'll be in an even worse mood if he catches you here.
I'm not scared of him.
Liar!
I've had enough of Jordan College. I feel as if I've been here forever.
Lord Asriel is coming. I wish he'd take me away with him.
Your uncle is even scarier than the Master.
Look!
?
Poison!
Are you mad?
Why are you always imagining things?
Come!
Let's go and greet Lord Asriel when he arrives.
Phew! It's a relief to stretch our legs!
Let's go!

OXFORD

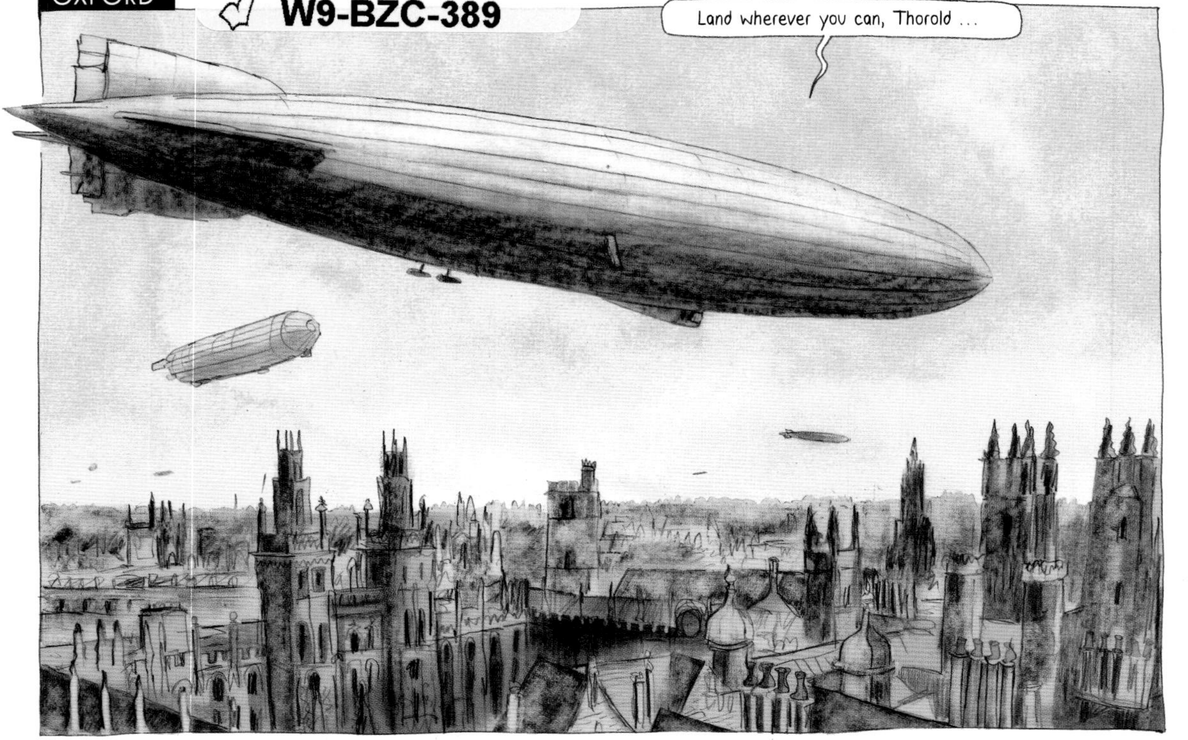
Land wherever you can, Thorold ...

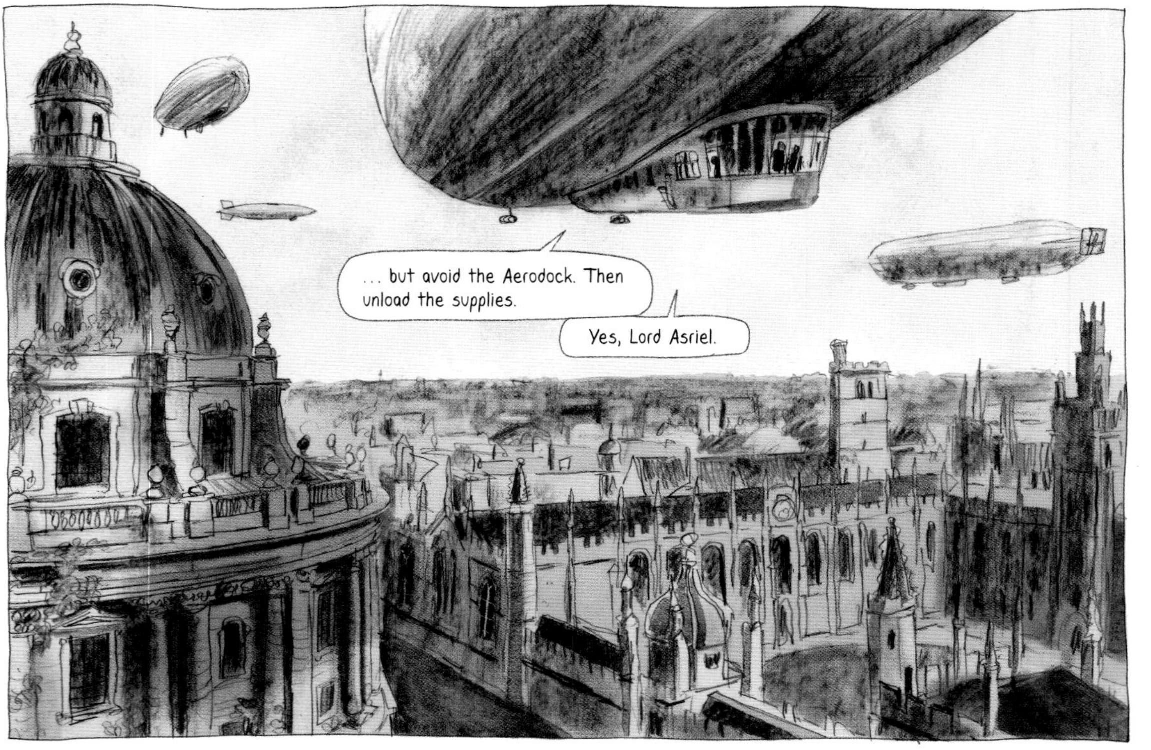
... but avoid the Aerodock. Then unload the supplies.
Yes, Lord Asriel.